A *Bride* FOR ALL *Seasons*

Would your perfect wedding be in the **spring**,
when flowers are starting to blossom and
it's the perfect season for new beginnings?

Or perhaps a balmy garden wedding,
set off by a riot of color, making the
summer bride glow with the joys of a happy future?

Do you dream of being a **fall** bride, walking down the aisle
amid the dazzling reds and burnished golds of falling leaves?

Or of a **winter** wedding dusted with glistening white
snowflakes, celebrated by the ringing of frosty church bells?

With Harlequin Romance® you can have them all!
And, best of all, you can experience the
rush of falling in love with a gorgeous groom....

In April we celebrated spring with:
The Bride's Baby
by **Liz Fielding**

Then we enjoyed the summer sun with:
Saying Yes to the Millionaire
by **Fiona Harper**

This month there's a whirlwind romance:
The Millionaire's Proposal
by **Trish Wylie**

Don't miss Christmas wedding bells:
Marry-Me Christmas
by **Shirley Jump**, out in December.

Visit http://abrideforallseasons.blogspot.com
to find out more....

"Close your eyes for me," she whispered, her voice seductively low and filled with emotion. *"Can you still see me?"*

He had to clear his throat to speak. "I can always see you. I told you that once before."

Since he'd met her, she was all he could see—in the daylight, when he couldn't stop looking at her, and when he was in the darkness, whether awake or on the fringes of sleep. She was all he saw.

He lifted one of her hands and set it flat against his chest, covering it with his own. "I see you with this. Your hair is a really deep chestnut, and it does this sexy, curly thing all around your face. Your eyes remind me of autumn. And you're smiling that way that makes it look like you're lit up from inside. I see you."

TRISH WYLIE

The Millionaire's Proposal

A *Bride* FOR ALL *Seasons*

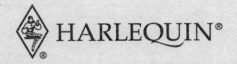

HARLEQUIN®

TORONTO • NEW YORK • LONDON
AMSTERDAM • PARIS • SYDNEY • HAMBURG
STOCKHOLM • ATHENS • TOKYO • MILAN • MADRID
PRAGUE • WARSAW • BUDAPEST • AUCKLAND

ISBN-13: 978-0-373-17540-6
ISBN-10:   0-373-17540-X

THE MILLIONAIRE'S PROPOSAL

First North American Publication 2008.

Copyright © 2008 by Trish Wylie.

This edition published by arrangement with Harlequin Books S.A.

® and TM are trademarks of the publisher. Trademarks indicated with ® are registered in the United States Patent and Trademark Office, the Canadian Trade Marks Office and in other countries.

www.eHarlequin.com

Printed in U.S.A.

Trish Wylie tried various careers before eventually fulfilling her dream of writing. Years spent working in the music industry, in promotions and teaching little kids about ponies gave her plenty of opportunity to study life and the people around her. Which, in Trish's opinion, is a pretty good study course for writing! Living in Ireland, Trish balances her time between writing and horses. If you get to spend your days doing things you love, then she thinks that's not doing too badly. You can contact Trish at www.trishwylie.com.

Praise for Trish Wylie

"Trish Wylie's *Bride of the Emerald Isle* is charming, witty and has a beautiful, unusual setting. It also has fantastic characters—particularly the wounded but wonderful Garrett."
—*Romantic Times BOOKreviews*

Trish also writes for Harlequin Presents

"*White-Hot!* is absolutely wonderful! Trish Wylie's spellbinding tale will tickle your funny bone and tug at your heartstrings. Featuring characters which leap off the pages, realistic dialogue, sweet romance, sizzling sex scenes, electrifying sexual tension and dramatic emotional intensity, *White-Hot!* is feel-good romance at its finest!"
—*Cataromance.com*

Dear Reader,

A good friend of mine reminded me of something important this year—to be grateful for the good stuff when it's here. How many of us dedicate the same amount of time to appreciating the good things as we do focusing on the bad? Maybe it's because the bad can be so very overwhelming, and over the years life simply wears us down. Yet it's the good stuff that makes the difference, don't you think?

We need to laugh as often as possible, take a deep breath of air to remind us we're alive, look around us and see the beauty in things, spend time doing what makes us happy. Most of all we need never get so old or so jaded that we stop dreaming or believing in moments of magic.

One of the things I love the absolute most about writing and reading romance is the fact it shows we all still believe in love in the twenty-first century. We may have busier lives, might be more cynical, but people still reach out for love in all its forms: in friends, in family, in a man and a woman who can make it through the rough times because life is richer together than it is apart. That's a little bit of magic right there.

So if there's one thing you bring with you out of Ronan and Kerry's story, I hope it's a little reminder to make the most of the good stuff and any moment of magic that comes your way. Grab hold of it, celebrate it, savour it, and that way even in times of darkness you'll still be able to see the light. Just like Ronan will with Kerry by his side.

Hs & Ks

Trish

CHAPTER ONE

KERRY DOYLE liked to consider herself a fairly patient woman. After all, she'd waited years to make her dream trip; researched, planned, scheduled everything to the nth degree. But if the man in the seat next to her poked her with his elbow one more time she thought she just might scream. She'd specifically allowed extra money for better seats on the longer flights for the added personal space that came with them. And it was a seven-hour flight from Dublin to New York—including the change at Shannon—one that was going to feel like twice that in the longer leg they were currently on if he didn't quit it soon.

And he'd shown so much promise in the 'scenery' department before he sat down too...

He poked her again, causing Kerry to let a sigh escape. It wasn't much of a poke—none of them had been—but even so...

'Sorry.'

It was a step in the right direction. 'Maybe if you sat a little more to the left?'

He turned in his seat, smiling at her with the kind of smile that probably worked wonders with the majority of women no matter how much he irritated them first. 'The stewardess already got me twice with the trolley. I'm not exactly built for these wee seats.'

All right, he had a point there. She hadn't been able to help noticing him when he got on the plane, especially when towering over her to place his bag in the overhead compartment. And he wasn't just scenic, he was tall—very tall. Not that she'd be able to guess accurately until she stood up and compared him to her own five seven, but if she had to hazard a guess she'd say he was well and truly over six feet tall. Add that to broad shoulders, a wide chest and muscled upper arms and even the fact that the rest of him seemed fairly lean wasn't going to help him fit into the space the airline had allocated, was it?

So she'd allow him that. She'd even sympathize a little, inwardly. 'No, you're not—but I'm just getting a little concerned about attempting to take a drink later in the flight if you bump me at the wrong time.'

It might also affect her choice of what she asked the stewardess for—after all, coffee and tea left stains. And the wardrobe she had with her had to last a long time. As always with Kerry it came down to practicalities—it was just the way her mind worked.

She accompanied her words with a polite smile in an attempt not to make an adversary for the rest of the flight, and then found herself suddenly distracted from further coherent thought by the way he examined her face before he replied.

Nice eyes. In fact he had *great* eyes. A pale blue made even paler when framed with thick dark lashes, which in turn highlighted the dark pools of his irises. Then there were shards of darker blue and white threaded through the paler blue—as if an artist's watercolour brush had been dipped into a glass of water and the colour hadn't quite mixed in yet. It was an unusual combination, and most definitely the kind of eyes a girl wouldn't forget in a hurry…

Kerry almost sighed again. For different reasons…

'Maybe we should set up some kind of a code?'

She dragged her gaze from his eyes long enough to note the hint of a smile on his devilishly sensual mouth. Well, having a sense of humour could only help with their predicament, so she allowed herself to smile a larger smile as she replied.

'Like me saying "Danger Will Robinson: drink approaching"?' And if he got that obscure reference to her childhood interest in truly bad nineteen sixties' science fiction she might have to love him a little.

'*Lost In Space*, right?'

Wow, he got it. She nodded, smiling a little brighter.

'Well, that would do it, all right. Or you could just dig me in the ribs every time I do it to you so I get a reminder about space of the personal variety.'

'That's certainly tempting.' Kerry's eyes narrowed as she pondered the 'temptation' involved in flirting with a complete stranger while travelling on the first leg of her grand adventure. Mind you, he was temptation personified—so who could really blame her? And even if he was dressed casually in jeans and a T-shirt just a shade or two darker than his sensational eyes, he *had* managed to afford to pay for better seating. That had to be a good sign.

Serial killers didn't travel in the good seats, she reckoned. Now kidnappers, well, *possibly*—the money was probably better…

His chin dropped and he leaned a little closer, employing a large hand to lift one side of her open book so he could read the cover, a hint of a smile hovering on the corners of his mesmerizing mouth.

'Enjoying the guidebook?'

Kerry turned it over on her tray table, grateful for the distraction, and nodding as she answered. 'So far—there's probably more detail in here than I need, though. I've read tonnes of them these last few months and this was one of the better ones.'

His dark brows quirked a minuscule amount when she glanced at him from the corner of her eye. 'More detail in what way?'

'Well, there's about a gazillion places listed in the back to begin with. And having never been there it's tough to decide what to see and what not when you're on a timescale, y'know?' Her gaze had locked fully with his again while she answered and a weird quiver of what almost felt like cold ran up her spine, goose-bumps appearing on her arms.

And when she felt like that it was normally an indication that she was clueing in on something—so what was it this time? Apart from the obvious feminine awareness of an incredibly good-looking male, that was.

She searched his face to see if she could figure it out. And even that was disconcerting. It was the proximity, she supposed. There was a certain intimacy to being seated beside someone on a plane. So the fact she was so aware of his breathing, the musky male undertone of his scent, the dark hint of stubble on his jaw, and each flicker of his thick lashes, was a completely natural reaction.

When she studied him a little longer than was probably considered polite, he turned his upper body in the seat and folded his arms across his broad chest.

'So how would you change it to make it more useful to you, then?'

What? Oh, yes, they'd been making polite conversation about the book, hadn't they? Kerry took a deep breath and looked back down at it, shaking her head a little at her uncharacteristic lack of being able to think straight. 'I dunno. Graded the chapters, maybe?'

'What way?'

'Length of stay? If you have two days you shouldn't miss this and that, a week you should try and see—that kind of thing.'

When she didn't get a reply she looked back up at him to discover a view of his profile, dark brows creased downwards in thought. He really was fascinating to look at, wasn't he? Not shaving-commercial good-looking, but certainly rugged enough to advertise outdoor wear or heavy duty Jeeps or maybe even activity holidays. He looked like a man's man and that meant he was automatically a woman's man too, didn't it? After all, there was something about a very male man that tugged at something deep inside a woman.

She was studying the short cropped dark chocolate of his hair when he snapped her out of her reverie…

'A list of things to pack for each length of trip might be useful too. Maybe a small section at the end of each chapter for whether you're a classical sightseer type or an adventurer or a party-goer or if you have kids along…that kind of thing…'

Kerry smiled indulgently as he mumbled to the back of the seat in front of him. 'Planning on rewriting the book now, are we?'

When he turned to look at her a smile danced in his eyes and she found herself mesmerized all over again before he hummed beneath his breath and answered with a softly spoken, 'Maybe.'

Unfolding his arms, he extended a large hand towards her. 'Ronan O'Keefe. And whatever you want to drink should really be on me to say thanks for buying a copy of my book. But as drinks are included I'll just have to promise not to make you spill anything.'

Kerry gaped, swiftly checked the name on the cover of the book, and then, rolling her eyes before shaking his hand, 'Just as well I didn't say anything too insulting about it, really, isn't it?'

And it explained the something she'd felt too. It'd been a forewarning of sorts, hadn't it?

Her hand enfolded firmly in the warmth of his long fingers, he held on just a little too long while fixing her gaze with his as he answered with a rumbling, 'Yes, it is.'

The warmth transferred to her smaller hand. He had the kind of firm handshake her father would have approved of and respected. But it wasn't quite respect Kerry was feeling. She even had to clear her throat before speaking.

'Would you have let on who you were if I had?'

'After a while.'

And the continuing sparkle in his eyes told her he'd have had fun with it too. 'Happened before, I take it?'

'Occupational hazard when travelling.' He inclined his head, 'I'm also incredibly good at recommending them to people in airport bookstores when I see them pick one up.'

When he added a lazy wink, Kerry couldn't help but laugh. Oh, he was a bit of a charmer, this one, wasn't he? Full of good old-fashioned Blarney, her nana would say with a throaty chuckle. He probably spent half his life chatting up women on planes, she wasn't anything special, which reminded her—it really was time she let go of his hand.

Gently extricating it, and immediately feeling the loss of warmth in contrast to the cool air from the plane's air-conditioning, she lifted her chin and challenged him with an upward arch of one brow,

'And how do I know you are who you say you are?'

'You could take my word for it?'

She turned her hand palm up and waggled her fingers, 'I might need to see your passport to be sure.'

'I might have a pen name.'

'Do you?'

'No.'

Her fingers waggled again.

'Not very trusting, are you?' He shook his head, working hard at keeping the smile twitching his mouth in check. 'Lesson one, by the way, would be: never give up your passport to a stranger when travelling alone.'

Her eyes narrowed. 'How do you know I'm travelling alone?'

'In my experience, people who travel together tend to sit together on planes.'

Good point. 'Well, it's not like I can grab your passport, climb over you and escape with it at twenty-seven thousand feet up, is it?'

'True—' he leaned a little closer and lowered his voice to a deliciously deep rumble '—though the climbing-over-me part might be fun to watch. No one's ever tried that before—brings a whole new meaning to the term "in-flight entertainment".'

When she heard the click of his seat belt and he leaned closer still, she automatically leaned back towards the window to make room for him. Not that it wasn't tempting to just stay where she was and 'sit' her ground, but this kind of dalliance was obviously something he was well practised at—and, Kerry being Kerry, she called him on it.

'Do you flirt with every woman you meet on a plane?'

Shooting her a challenging quirk of his brows as he reached behind him, he replied with, 'Would make for lots of short relationships, don't you think?'

'Another occupational hazard, perchance?'

'Possibly.'

The contortions eventually wielded a well-worn passport he waved back in front of her face as he got comfy again. 'I need this back. So be warned—I'll wrestle you for it if I have to.'

'Duly noted.' She reached for it, but Ronan moved it just out of her reach.

'Let's make a fair exchange.'

'Oh-h-h,' Kerry laughed throatily, 'I don't think so.'

'Picture that bad?'

'Are you suggesting I don't photograph well?'

He examined her face for a moment, the same low intimacy returning to his voice. 'I doubt it.'

Kerry felt warmth building on her cheeks, which she'd always thought for a woman her age was just plain old sad. That very thought then bringing her in a straight line to her excuse.

'Didn't anyone tell you not to ask a lady her age?'

He frowned in amused confusion, tapping his passport off the knuckles of his hand. 'And when did I do that?'

'My date of birth is in my passport.'

'Ah…'

'And anyway, you have an aisle seat—you could make a faster getaway. Someone told me recently that giving your passport to a stranger is a bad idea when travelling alone.'

There was a low chuckle of very male laughter, the sound making her smile at him again. Should she have to hazard a guess, Kerry would say that the 'flirting with women on planes' thing was pretty successful for him. Maybe the short relationships suited his lifestyle?

'Do I get a name?'

She spoke slowly, 'You already *have* a name, Ronan.'

'*Your* name.'

'We'll see…' She waggled her fingers again.

His stunning eyes narrowed briefly, the passport still tapping against his large hand. 'I'll swap you a look at my passport for your name.'

'Once I've confirmed you are who you say you are, I'll reveal my secret identity—how does that sound?'

'*That*—' he smiled again, forcing another smile from her in response before he added '—is a deal.'

When her fingers closed around the end of the proffered

passport he held on, waiting for her lashes to lift before adding, 'And I'm not the only one capable of a little flirting on a plane, am I?'

Tugging it free, she informed him with a haughty lift of her nose, 'You obviously bring out my dark side.'

'Not sure I'd agree with that.'

Kerry shook her head, dropping her chin to flip through the passport and discovering page after page of stamps from varying countries around the globe. 'Have you really been to all these places?'

'Nah, I make my own stamps—it's a hobby of mine.' He chuckled again when she glared at him. 'It's easier to write a travel guide for a country if you've been there, I find. I tried it from home but no one ever came to visit my kitchen after I wrote the guide for there—which is a shame really, 'cos I had some great package deals going.'

Kerry continued reading all the country names, trying to imagine what it must have been like to have visited so many places and seen so many things. It had to have made for an exciting life; he'd make one heck of a dinner guest. And it was yet another thing she could find attractive about him, because even if their 'relationship' was only going to last for the duration of the flight, she had to admit he was pretty irresistible on many levels—full of charm, in possession of a fully working sense of humour, capable of giving as good as he got, sexy as sin…a walking fountain of knowledge when it came to travelling…

Be silly not to take advantage of the latter, really.

When she found the photograph page she laughed softly. 'Oh, dear—now that's bad.'

Ronan leaned in to look over her shoulder, his upper arm pressed against her shoulder. 'Just needs a row of numbers across the bottom, doesn't it? And a couple of shots from either side to make up the set.'

Kerry turned her face towards his, her gaze searching his eyes back and forth while she breathed in deep breaths of his scent. 'Voice of experience?'

His smile was slow and oozing with blatantly male sexuality, the brush of thick lashes against tanned skin deliberately slow, she was certain. And when he spoke it was with that deep, rumbling, intimate tone again, the air between them seeming to vibrate and—well—sizzle a little, frankly.

'Not in that area, no,' he stage-whispered, 'but I did get detention after school on a pretty regular basis. Just don't tell anyone in case it affects my ability to get into some countries, okay?'

'Your secret's safe with me.'

When she answered in an equally low stage whisper, her gaze tangled with his again, a shiver of something running up her spine, radiating outwards, leaving her skin tingling and a strange tightness in her chest.

What was that? She'd never been so very aware of a man on such a cellular level before and it was—a little unsettling, actually.

'Could I ask you to put your tray down, please, sir?'

The voice of a stewardess broke the charged silence, forcing Ronan back into his allocated space before he lowered his tray, a smile aimed up at the pretty blonde as she served him his meal. He wasn't the least bit tempted to flirt with her, he noticed, not the way he had with the woman beside him. It was something unusual for him—not that he hadn't been known to make small talk with someone on a long-haul flight if they hadn't handed out the usual 'leave me alone' signals of burying their nose in a paperback or plugging in headphones.

But she was—intriguing, he supposed was the right word. What was someone like her doing travelling alone? No rings anywhere, he'd noted, so it would be a boyfriend rather than husband meeting her in New York if there was one. But something told him there wasn't either one or she wouldn't be flirting back with him the way she was. Women who blushed as prettily as she had weren't players in that league, were they?

Business trip, then—visiting friends maybe.

Only one way to find out, so once they had their meals in front of them he turned his head to look at her again. 'What takes you to the Big Apple?'

She handed him his passport, which he tucked between his thighs without removing his gaze from her face. She should be well used to men looking at her, as pretty as she was with gleaming chestnut hair waving around her fine features and the full mouth with a constant upward curve suggesting she smiled more often than not.

'It's on my fantasy list.'

It took considerable effort to keep a strangled edge out of his voice. 'Your *what?*'

Because his furtive imagination had just gone straight to Sinville with that one.

'Kind of like fantasy football only with destinations instead of players.' She nodded, tucking a strand of richly coloured hair behind her ear so he could see a small earring dangling against the skin of her neck as she leaned forward to examine what was on her tray—the simple sight intensely sensual. 'I've spent so long burying myself in work that this trip is made up entirely of places off the top of the list.'

Ronan watched as she flashed him a sideways glance and a small smile that warmed the hints of russet in her large brown eyes.

'I'm going round the world.'

And the husky sense of satisfaction in her voice was a pleasure to his ears. 'Alone?'

'Now, if you were me would you answer that question when a stranger asked it?'

'No.'

She nodded again, ripping the plastic off her utensils. 'There you go, then.'

'So are you?'

She turned her shoulders and fixed him with a steady 'straight in the eye' gaze. 'Now, Mr O'Keefe—'

'Oh, no, you don't.' He leaned a little closer—something he'd been doing a lot of the last few minutes. 'I was Ronan five minutes ago—and *you* owe *me* a name.'

'That was before you threatened me with a knife.'

When she dipped her chin in the direction of his hand he looked down, then back. 'It's a three-inch plastic knife—I'd say you're safe from any lasting harm, wouldn't you?'

When she continued to challenge him with her steady gaze and a minuscule quirk of her perfectly arched brows he took a deep breath and set the utensils down, replacing them with a spoon and the dessert tub, which he automatically ripped the cover off.

Her eyes widened. 'You're eating dessert first?'

'Yup,' he answered with his mouth full of a surprisingly good lemon cheesecake, mentally making a note of it in association with the airline. 'Why wait for the good stuff? Life's too short.'

'That's profound. But I think you'll find it has more to do with the savoury-before-sweet rule.'

There was a brief pause while Ronan studied her, cheesecake dissolving on his tongue. 'There's a rule?'

'Yes, and for good reason.'

'Never was one for following rules.'

'I can believe that.'

Ronan sat a little taller, because he was quite proud of his reputation as a rule-breaker, as it happened. He'd never been one for accepting the going odds either. And he wasn't that easily distracted.

'*Name.*'

She laughed, the sound amazingly sexy in the intimate space between them, and Ronan had been on more planes than he could count on his fingers and toes combined and never once had he found himself wishing the flight could be a few hours longer than it actually was.

'Does it matter? Not like you'll ever see me again after this flight touches down.'

'We made a deal.' And as a rule-follower she wasn't likely to go back on a deal, was she?

She ran the rosy tip of her tongue over her full lips, bringing Ronan's gaze to her mouth as she formed the words.

'It's Kerry, Kerry Doyle.'

It suited her, was—*right* somehow. 'Nice to meet you, Kerry, Kerry Doyle.'

And her mouth curled into an answering wide smile that showed straight teeth and mischievous dimples—oh, she was really something.

'Funny guy.'

Trailing his gaze from her mouth to the warmth of her eyes, and then somewhat reluctantly for the first time in his life to focus on his dessert, he silently cleared his throat before digging a little deeper to satisfy his raging curiosity.

'Tell me more about this fantasy list.'

'Is it a good idea for a woman travelling alone to give her itinerary to a stranger on a plane?'

Actually he wasn't entirely convinced that was the kind of fantasies he'd meant, his mouth curling into a lazy smile at the thought as he loaded his spoon. 'We've just been introduced so technically we're not strangers any more—just as well, too, seeing you've just confirmed you're travelling alone.'

When a quick turn of his head afforded him a glimpse of a recriminating frown he grinned inwardly. 'Don't look a gift horse and all that. You have a bonafide destination expert literally at your fingertips—feel free to take advantage of me.'

He threw in another wink for good measure.

'Oh, you just don't quit, do you?'

'Being helpful? Can't say women list that as my most memorable quality, no.'

'*Flirting.*'

'Ah.' It took considerable effort to hold the full-blown smile he could feel in his chest from making its way up onto his face. 'Well, you do know they say it's all about the individual's interpretation.'

Kerry laughed a low, husky laugh. 'You're incorrigible.'

'I've been told. Tell me about your trip, then.'

She did, over 'dinner', through coffee that didn't get spilt thanks to the code they had in place, and she even produced a colour-coded itinerary Ronan found highly amusing as she explained it to him while they ignored the movie. It was as they began their descent into JFK that he explained to her the treasures that could be found if she didn't limit herself to the usual sights that would swallow up great chunks of her time when she was stuck in huge lines of tourists all wanting to see the same things—Kerry scribbling notes into the margins of her neatly typed sheets of paper.

Her enthusiasm was palpable, watching the thoughts crossing her expressive eyes was addictive—and Ronan found himself regretting again the fact he hadn't met her in Dublin on the first leg of the flight.

'It must be amazing to spend your life seeing all the places you see.'

An innocuous statement, but the words twisted like a knife in his chest. 'Yeah, it's been great.'

Placing her itinerary with its brand new scribbled notes into a Ziploc bag, she leaned back against her seat and sighed, a small, contented smile on her mouth and a faraway look in her eyes as she turned her face towards his watchful gaze, her voice low.

'I can't imagine half the things you've seen—you're incredibly lucky.'

Lucky was far from the mark, as it happened. But Ronan's imagination was too busy deciding that, with both their heads against the headrests and their faces turned towards each other, it was too much as if they were lying side by side in a bed for him to descend into bitterness—his voice husky as a result of where his brain then took that mental image.

'Have you got everything on your fantasy list covered or is there anything else I can help you with?'

She chuckled, letting the innuendo slide. 'This trip is just the beginning. I've got almost three months to pack in as much as I can, so it's a taster, if you like. Then if there's anywhere I really enjoy I'll try and spend more time there next time round.'

She had dozens more adventures to look forward to. And enthusiasm danced in her eyes, highlighting the hinted shades of russet and gold in amongst the brown—though his imagination was probably filling that in...

She really couldn't be any more different from him if she tried, could she? But he managed to keep the envy out of his voice, just. 'I can recommend some great guidebooks to help you catch up with me, if you like.'

Kerry laughed the soft laugh he found so enthralling. 'I'll just bet you can. Do you have one for the first-time traveller? You know—with all those tips about never confessing you're travelling alone, or why not to give your name to strangers on planes and that one about the passport? They're all very useful.'

'And you ignored every single one of them—' he couldn't help smiling when she did '—though I'm glad you did 'cos, between you and me, this has been the shortest Atlantic crossing I've ever had.'

After only a moment's hesitation she leaned a little closer to whisper, 'You're welcome.'

He couldn't stop looking into her eyes. Searching each of them closely, with the sense of intimacy rising as he felt the soft wisp of her warm breath against his face. And the urge to kiss her was so strong when the cabin lights dimmed and his vision blurred that it was as physical a need to him as the one for oxygen.

He'd only have to lean just a little bit closer…

There was a jolt as the large plane touched down, a ripple of applause working its way through the cabin and making Kerry laugh again as she moved back and arched up to look over the seat in front of her.

'Okay—is it unusual for a pilot to actually land the plane safely here?'

When the cabin lights flickered back on Ronan eventually dragged his gaze upwards from where he'd been attempting to fill his eyes with the sight of her lithe body arched against her seat belt.

'It was a smooth landing.' He shrugged. 'Sometimes folks just think that merits a thank-you.'

'I'll remember that for next time.'

She had dozens of next times ahead of her, didn't she? With an unaccustomed wave of angry bitterness, Ronan thought he should make sure and clap whenever he touched down in Dublin again—a kind of 'thanks for the memories' to all the pilots who'd got him from one place to the other in the last decade.

Kerry settled back in her seat, took a deep breath and asked, 'How long are you in New York for?'

'Why?'

The words came out in a rush. 'I don't suppose I can persuade you to play tour guide for a day?'

It wasn't going to take much persuasion.

CHAPTER TWO

KAREN had to be losing her tiny mind.

Since when did she run around asking men she'd only just met to spend a day with her? Since never—that was when. It wasn't that she was stuck in some old-fashioned notion that a woman didn't have as much a right to ask a man out as the other way round, but it wasn't something she made a habit of. And what did she really know about this guy beyond the fact he was disgustingly good-looking, great company and more than a little fascinating to her?

She swiped her clammy palms along the sides of her crisp white shorts and pushed her sunglasses up onto her head, squinting as she looked around the crowded street. If he stood her up that would be one way of getting out of it, she supposed. But the truth was she didn't want him to stand her up—the idea of another day in his company having been sending a flutter of anticipation through her stomach since before she'd gone to sleep the night before. And she couldn't remember the last time she'd felt that before seeing a man. Not that it was a date, because it wasn't—she'd even offered to pay him for acting as her tour guide.

He'd laughed, mind you.

But it still wasn't a date. It was a stolen day, a one-off, a way of marking her newfound freedom by doing something completely out of character...

Lord, but it was hot. She really hadn't been prepared for how hot it was, or how heavy the air was, or how sticky and dishevelled she felt or how noisy and overwhelming New York was with the constant sound of car horns and the wail of sirens echoing from streets away or the number of people or—

Her breath catching when she saw him.

He was standing in the midst of all the people milling around in front of the Empire State Building and it was just plain daft that in that moment he was the only thing Kerry could see. It was simply that he was the only familiar face, was all. And, as much as she'd told herself she was fine with making such a large trip alone, the truth was some of the joy of her first night in New York had been tempered by the fact she had no one with her to turn to and share it with. Like the excitement of the first moment she saw the Manhattan skyline laid out in front of her, and it finally hit her that she was *in New York*!

She continued staring at Ronan, reasoning again that no one could really blame her—he was incredibly easy on the eyes. Standing with his feet spread, as if claiming the small piece of sidewalk underneath him, he had his hands on his lean hips while he slowly turned a circle, searching the crowd with a frown of concentration on his face. The bright sunlight made his short, spiking hair look lighter—a milk chocolate as opposed to the dark she'd thought it was on the plane—and he just looked so, so, well, he *did*.

Kerry raised a hand and waved it above her head.

But Ronan continued circling, so, feeling a little silly for waving like an idiot, she walked forwards, swiping her hands down her sides again as she got closer. 'Hi there—do you by any chance know how to get to the Empire State Building?'

The lazy smile that slid onto his mouth brought an immediate answering smile to her lips. How pathetic was it she was glad to see him? And it didn't bode too well for her conviction she could take her trip alone and still enjoy it just as much, did it?

'You're close, if it helps any.'

Stopping a foot away from him, she watched as his gaze travelled down her body all the way to her feet before rising faster than it had lowered. And she was surprised by how the simple glance suddenly made her feel warmer than she already was, every nerve ending tingling with awareness.

'So are we starting the grand tour here?'

Ronan casually pushed his large hands into his jeans pockets, adopting the pose of a man extremely comfortable in his own skin. 'Is there a queue all the way round the block?'

Kerry turned on her heel and surveyed the long line of people, sometimes three or four deep, stretching from the entrance until they disappeared around the corner; the thought of joining the end of a line that length in the sweltering heat was enough to draw a small groan from her lips.

'Yes.'

'Then no.' He shot a glance at the bag resting on her hip, the strap slung diagonally across her body between her breasts. 'I suppose you have the obligatory camera in there for pictures of all the sights?'

Kerry patted it with one hand, her chin rising with confidence. 'And sun cream and a mini-fan and a bottle of water and a map and energy bars and a mobile phone and—'

Ronan smiled wryly, long fingers wrapping around her elbow to turn her before he started walking into the crowd. 'Well at least if we get stranded in the desert we'll survive.'

'Are you making fun of the fact I like to be prepared for every eventuality, Mr O'Keefe?'

'Possibly. But if I achieve nothing else today it's my aim to sway you towards the merits of travelling light—I saw how much luggage you took off that carousel yesterday. And unless

I'm very much mistaken, this is supposed to be a fun experience for you—not an endurance test.'

Kerry felt the skin on her elbow tingling beneath his hand, warmth travelling like an electric current up her arm, over her shoulder and downwards towards her breasts, disconcerting enough for her to feel the need to gently twist free of his touch before it worked its way anywhere else. Then she felt the need to lessen the small rejection with a sidewards glance and a pout of her lower lip.

'I *need* all those clothes. It's a trip through two seasons and half a dozen countries—and that involves a varied wardrobe. And anyway, I only have the absolute necessities with me.'

Ronan sounded unconvinced. 'Your idea of bare necessities and mine aren't the same, I'd guess.'

'That's because you're a man and I'm a woman.'

'No—it's because I'm a seasoned traveller and you're a virgin.'

Kerry couldn't help making a small derisive snort.

And it was enough to make Ronan turn his head to look down at her face, his voice threaded with the cheek of the devil. 'In travelling terms anyway. Because obviously by your age and looking the way you do…'

Her jaw dropped.

But he merely chuckled and reclaimed her elbow to steer her closer to the kerb. 'Okay, Kerry, Kerry Doyle, I'm prepared to give a little on the traditional tourist stuff for the first hour or so to give you some quick photo op's seeing you're on a tight schedule—plus this is an easy way to get your bearings, so—'

'What is?'

He quirked his brows at her in barely disguised amusement, then jerked a thumb over his shoulder and added the words slowly as if he were talking to a complete idiot. '*That is.*'

Kerry was a tad bemused, folding her arms across her

breasts and blinking up at him before she asked, 'Mr Great Adventurer is putting me on an open-top bus with the rest of the tourists? My, my, aren't you the daring one? I'm so glad I have travel insurance.'

'We can take the subway and boil to death if you prefer. You won't see as much, mind you…'

Hard as it was to believe that anywhere barring the face of the sun could be any hotter than where she already was, and with him looking at her the way he was, Kerry wasn't prepared to find out. But she was a little disappointed—she could have found one of the many bus tours on her own. Somehow she'd expected more from Ronan. Had maybe secretly hoped for more? And that some of that sense of adventure might rub off on her?

He stepped closer and bent his knees until he was looking her directly in the eye, his proximity doing things to her pulse rate and breathing that she hadn't experienced since, well, since the plane, actually…

'Trust me.' His voice dropped seductively, the vibration of the deep tone reaching out to interrupt the usual rhythm of her heart. 'I promise you won't forget today.'

Kerry swallowed. She believed him—but somehow she knew, deep to the pit of her soul, it wouldn't just be the sight-seeing she'd remember. And that was a strangely scary thought. Especially when she'd spent so long waiting for a time in her life when she finally had her independence; she'd fought long and hard, worked more hours than she cared to think about, had constantly put the needs of others first. Not that she wanted to change that—but the last thing she needed was to get even temporarily attached to someone who was probably as reliable as an Irish summer.

'Can I ask you a question?'

He stood tall again, towering over her by a good six inches. 'Depends.'

'How many women you meet on planes end up asking you to play tour guide for them?'

'Regretting asking?'

'Curious.'

He folded his arms across his chest, mirroring her stance, the simple action accenting the muscles in his forearms and biceps. 'About how often I do this or why you asked me in the first place?'

'Yes.'

And why he'd agreed, she supposed. Not that she needed her ego stroked, but she was curious as to why he'd said yes as quickly as he had. He had to be in New York for a reason, didn't he? Meeting with a publisher? More research for a new book maybe? Someone who'd travelled as much as he had didn't make a trip just for the sake of it, did they? And if that was the case had he dropped whatever he was doing in favour of spending the day with her?

Because she really wouldn't want him to think that she'd repay him at the end of it with—or that he was onto some kind of a sure thing or—

'First up, let's remember you asked me and not the other way round—though I'd have offered if you'd given me five minutes. Or at the very least pointed you in the general direction of some of my favourite places.'

Kerry opened her mouth.

But Ronan wasn't done. 'Secondly, I don't tend to talk to people on planes much—and any I've bothered with have never been a beautiful woman travelling alone, more's the pity. So, yes—you're the first one for a guided tour. I'm only human.'

Of all the very many things in there she could have picked to ask questions on, Kerry's brain could only seem to focus on the one thing: he thought she was beautiful. Really? Not pretty or cute but honest-to-goodness beautiful?

It made her positively glow—a guy like *him* thinking that. So much for not needing her ego stroked.

'Thirdly—' he took a measured breath that expanded his wide chest before continuing with an almost reluctant tone in his voice, as if he wasn't completely comfortable saying the words '—I guess the idea of seeing things through your eyes appealed to me. It'll do me good to see it from a new perspective—who knows? I might even get a chapter of a book out of it. I'll even promise to give you an acknowledgement if I do.'

He recovered with a wink. 'You can *thank me later…*'

'Ronan—' But before she could find anything coherent to say there was a loud greeting from the upper floor of the bus.

'Ro—my man! C'mon up.'

Ronan grinned, tilting his head right back to throw an answer back. 'Hey, Johnnie boy—you save us the good seats?'

'Uh-huh. That your friend?'

'Yup.'

The younger man whistled. 'She's way too good-lookin' for you, old man—bring her up here so I can steal her away.'

Kerry laughed when the words were accompanied with an exaggerated wink and a beckoning index finger. 'And *that* is?'

Ronan cupped her elbow again, guiding her onto the bus as he leaned his head down, lowering his voice to a conspiratorial whisper.

'Best tour guide in New York City—just don't go telling him I said so or he'll be unbearable.' He stood taller, voice rising a little. 'These tours are all about the guides; get a local like John and you'll get more insight about the city and the best places to go than you ever would from a book.'

Kerry lowered her voice to the same conspiratorial level he'd used. 'Don't you know someone who could maybe *put it* in a book?'

'Ah-h-h, but these stories aren't mine to tell—they're his. And no two tours are ever the same with John. There's always something new to add or a different joke or something that happened the day before. And that's what travelling is all about—the people as much as the places. Some places you might forget, but you won't forget the people you met along the way. Memories Kerry, Kerry Doyle—yours, the people you meet's—that's what you'll have at the end of every trip you take. Moments; snapshots in time, if you like.'

They paused at the bottom of narrow metal stairs leading to the upper deck, where Ronan released her arm and Kerry felt the rush of air-conditioned coolness wash over the heated brand of his touch, creating goose-bumps on her skin. But even though she was aware of it, it was the wistfulness in his voice as he painted the romantic picture that captured her attention most, echoing a need inside her for the kind of moments he'd just described.

'You really love what you do, don't you?'

The sigh was silent, but she caught it. What was it that suddenly made him frown? Why did he turn away from her and look up the stairs as if he didn't want to look her in the eye? And why did she suddenly feel so ridiculously—*sad* somehow? She really wished she could place a mental finger on whatever it was.

He was quite the mystery.

'I did.'

Kerry wasn't completely sure she'd heard him say it, but before she could check a pair of feet appeared on the stairs and an upturned palm was offered her way.

'Come on up, sweet thing. I have a seat saved specially for *you*—Ro can just stay down there.'

'And leave her with you? Don't think so, pal.'

'*Ro?*' Picking on the nickname she'd previously ignored, she shot an amused glance at Ronan.

'Don't even think about adopting it. I can leave you stranded somewhere. Or with Johnnie—he's famous with the ladies, so if you prefer…'

Placing her hand into John's, she leaned back a little while walking up the steps. 'I think I'll stick with the devil I know.'

She'd always been a sucker for a mystery.

Ronan had spent half a day with her and he still didn't get her. Not that he'd ever felt the need to place people in boxes so he knew where he stood in the world, but normally he was a good judge—he was worldly-wise, after all. But her he just didn't get.

For starters he found it hard to believe someone like her didn't have a load of friends who could've gone on holiday with her. Not that everyone could take three months off work to travel round the world, but still. That thought process then led him to wonder what she did that allowed *her* to take three months off work. She was a little mature for a student taking a gap. He put her early thirties maybe—though she could have passed for younger—but she had a maturity and intelligence to the way she spoke and acted that made him believe she had some life experience under her belt. People over the age of thirty were—calmer, he supposed. They knew what they wanted, were less worried about what people thought, more 'together'.

And as the day progressed he couldn't help wondering something else: how she'd managed to stay single when she looked the way she did. Because he wasn't the only one looking at her as if she were the last female left on the planet, was he?

John flirted outrageously with her during the tour and although Kerry didn't overly play up to it she hadn't exactly discouraged him either; laughing that husky laugh of hers, her lips parting to draw in the odd gasp at his audacity when he made innuendos over the tannoy and then blushing adoringly straight after, eyes shining. And it had bugged Ronan, frankly. He didn't want Johnnie-boy to be the one getting all those reactions.

Almost as if somewhere in his mind Ronan had claimed her as his for the day.

She made a small moaning sound beside him and stretched long, slender legs directly into his line of vision, so he turned his head to watch as she stretched the rest of her body. And had to stifle a groan when his body reacted in a very swift, very male way to what he saw—the woman should wear a warning!

She'd clasped the fingers of one hand around the wrist of the other before lifting her arms above her head and had her head tilted back, eyes closed as she let the sun warm her face. And the combined stretching of legs and arms had arched her spine off the bench, her breasts straining against the snug fit of her azure-blue vest-top.

'I am *so* hot.'

Ronan couldn't help but silently agree.

'Is it normally this hot here this time of year?'

When she resumed a normal sitting position he just about managed to look at her face before she opened her eyes. 'They're having a heatwave. But it's probably the humidity you're feeling. We Irish aren't used to it. You'll adjust in a couple of days.'

'A couple of days before I move on then—don't s'pose you know what the weather is like in Canada?'

He cocked a brow and she smiled.

'Okay—yes, you do.' She rolled her eyes while reaching out for the iced water they'd bought from one of the street vendors who'd happily tossed it to the upper floor of the bus in exchange for a scrunched-up dollar bill thrown down at them. Something that had entertained her immensely at the time.

'I keep forgetting this is all old hat for you. I must look like a little kid on Christmas morning.'

Yeah, she did. But he liked that about her. He'd soaked up some of her enthusiasm as she took in everything on the tour, and the number of times she'd gently set her fine-boned hand on his arm to get his attention before pointing at something or leaned across him to get a better photograph of the Flat Iron

Building or the Courthouse or the Woolworth Building or City Hall had only added to his overall enjoyment.

Somewhere along the way he'd forgotten what it was like to feel so excited about everything. But, as good as it was to be reminded not to take things for granted just because he'd seen them a thousand times, it was also a little like poking an open wound with a stick; reminding him of the dark thoughts he'd been putting to the back of his mind the last few months— which had been a bit tough to take, and left him pensive.

What he needed was a way to lighten his mood, and to stop him obsessing about Kerry's 'hot' body.

He turned his head and focussed on the kids playing in front of them. At the bottom end of the island of Manhattan, Battery Park was packed the way it always was, hundreds of tourists milling around filling in time while they took turns patiently waiting in the mile-long queue weaving its way along the concrete paths to the ferries for Ellis and Liberty Islands.

The kids between them and the incoming ferries had the right idea in the heat, Ronan reckoned—in fact…

He grinned, taking Kerry's hand before standing up and tugging to get her off the bench. 'C'mon.'

'Where are—?'

'You said you were hot, right?'

She resisted, dragging her feet while trying to open her bag and stow away her water, a curtain of hair hiding their destination until it was too late, 'I did and I am but—'

She squeaked when the narrow fountain of water appeared directly in front of her feet, shooting high enough above her head to sprinkle her face on the downward journey. And Ronan chuckled at the look of surprise on her face, deliberately stepping back so another jet appeared beside them.

Kerry's eyes narrowed.

He shrugged. 'Cooler now, aren't you?'

For a moment she simply glared at him. And then she

caught him off guard by moving neatly to one side and tugging on his hand so he was stood pretty much directly over the next jet of water when it appeared.

Closing his eyes, he pursed his lips and shook his head hard to get the water off his hair. Then he opened his eyes, looked down to locate another of the metal rings, and when she tried to tug her hand free he closed his fingers tighter, hauling her forwards and smiling at her gasp as her breasts hit the wall of his chest.

She shook her hair out of her eyes, looked up at him with wide eyes and then laughed as he smirked and spun her—once, twice, in and out of several jets of cold water before releasing her without warning and swinging her out to arm's length where she was promptly soaked from head to toe by fountains either side of her. Only then did he allow her fingers to slip free from his, deliberately slow so they touched fingertip to fingertip for a few seconds before both their arms dropped.

He prepared himself for outrage.

But before his captivated gaze she simply tilted her head to one side, quirked an arched brow, and deliberately skipped sideways underneath another jet.

Ronan laughed, feeling an inner lightness returning to his chest that'd been missing for longer than he cared to admit. So he made a sideways slide in the opposite direction to her skip—and got wet.

Kerry checked the ground, made a skip back and to her left and got wetter still, lifting her arms from her sides and leaning her head back to welcome the cooling spray. Then she turned round and round in slow circles getting wetter and wetter as each plume of water appeared, her effervescent laughter drawing answering, somewhat lower laughter from Ronan as he watched.

She was amazing. He wondered if she knew that. Somehow he doubted *he'd* forget it. And, having talked to her briefly about 'moments', he knew he was experiencing one of them right there and then…

Kerry laughed at the sheer ridiculousness of what she was doing. What was it they said about people shedding their inhibitions when away from home ground? But it wasn't just that. She was having fun. Honest-to-goodness *fun*—joy bubbling up inside her like bubbles in a flute of champagne.

She was in New York, on the first leg of a dream of a lifetime and to top it off she was messing around with an incredibly sexy guy under a set of fountains in the bright sunshine in Battery Park. Life didn't get much better than that, she reckoned.

They managed to get wet another couple of times on their way out, both still grinning from the shared experience as they walked through the crowd and Kerry fully aware, but not the least bit bothered, by the amused looks aimed their way.

She shook droplets of moisture off her arms and lifted her hands to her hair—ruffling it in the vain hope the hot midday sun would dry it into something resembling curls rather than a frizzy mess. She then stole a sideways glance at Ronan, who was flapping the end of his white T-shirt back and forth, no doubt to try and dry it some—not that Kerry actually had a problem with it plastered against his well-defined chest.

And when he turned his head to look at her she felt her breath catch again, the way it had when she'd spotted him in the crowd. He really did do incredible things to her pulse rate, didn't he? She'd never met anyone who could do that—and so effortlessly too. He had only to breathe in and out and she found it completely fascinating.

They laughed.

'Well, you're cooler now, aren't you?' He nudged his upper arm off her shoulder.

So she nudged him back a little harder, laughing all the more when he made an exaggerated stagger to the side. 'You're a big kid, you know that, don't you?'

A large hand was slapped against his chest. 'Me? I'll have you know I'm the responsible one—I just made sure the chances of you getting heatstroke were lessened. You're the one who turned it into a game.'

Still smiling, but with her gaze now fixed forwards on the poignant sight of the mounted globe salvaged from Ground Zero, Kerry admitted in a soft voice, 'It was fun.'

She dropped her chin to study the painted toenails visible in her sandalled feet for a moment before giving in to the need to look back at Ronan, who was looking at her with a strangely intense expression on his face.

'You make it sound like it's something you don't normally make time for.'

She scrunched up her nose.

'How come?'

Spoken by the man who was as free as a bird to the woman who'd been trapped by responsibility for over a decade. 'I have fun. I just don't—'

'Have fun the way you just did?'

Normally the lack of smart suits and forcefully tamed hair was enough to fool the world into thinking she was more carefree than she actually was. And he hadn't seen her in work clothes, so, 'Do I look boring?'

'No, that's why I'm surprised—and now curious.'

Kerry liked that she could make him curious. In the short time she'd known him Lord alone knew there'd been plenty of things that had her curious about *him*, so it was a good feeling to be able to return the favour.

When she didn't speak he asked the obvious. 'So what holds you back?'

'Is therapy a complimentary part of the tour?'

'Ooh—*defensive*.'

How had he done that? Having used the gentle tone he just had, he'd made her feel guilty for not spilling her guts. And

Kerry never did, well, not unless she'd known someone a really long time, which technically made it a moot point because anyone who'd known her that long already *knew*.

But she wasn't going to ruin such an amazing day with a conversation examining the psychology of why she was the way she was in normal everyday life. So she brushed it over by nudging her shoulder against his arm again, lifting her other hand to push her fingers into the hair on top of her head and ruffling it before letting it fall.

'What's next? I assume from your previous disdain for people with patience that we're not joining the longest queue in the history of mankind so we can make some kind of Irish pilgrimage to Ellis…'

The low rumble of laughter reassured her she'd managed to brush over what could have been an awkward moment. 'You'd be correct in that assumption. But I do need to know how you feel about boats.'

Kerry stopped and turned to face him, considering a random point above his left ear while she answered. 'Kinda depends if we're talking rowboat or cruise ship here. Though I should warn you I hadn't planned on the cruise portion of my fantasy list for another twenty years or so. And I was thinking more along the lines of the Caribbean for that one.'

'I'm sure you'll enjoy that. But I'm thinking more along the lines of the Staten Island ferry. You can see Ellis and take some pictures of Liberty while I fill you in on the associated history free of charge—I'm helpful that way.'

Her gaze shifted to lock with his, the smile immediate and reciprocated just as fast. 'Lead on Macduff.'

He stared at her for a long moment, searching her eyes while a dozen thoughts crossed through the varying shades of blue in his. But just when she thought he might say something else, he laced his fingers with hers and tugged.

'C'mon then, Kerry, Kerry Doyle.'

The invisible angelic midget on one shoulder said she really shouldn't allow him to keep touching her the way he did; as if he had a right to do it and had been doing it for ever. But the equally small invisible siren in high heels on her other promptly reminded her she'd been just as keen to touch *him* on the bus tour. And fair was fair.

So she decided for just one day of her life she wasn't going to over-think. She was simply going to do things because she wanted to and because they felt right. Not because she was expected to behave a certain way or because she was concerned what other people thought—the trip was the first thing she'd specifically done for herself in a long, long time, after all. And she'd earned it; she didn't have to feel guilty about *anything*.

If karma was going to punish her for grabbing hold of one perfect day, then let it try—they'd be having a long talk about time served.

So she tangled her fingers a little firmer around Ronan's—softening any subliminal meaning he might get from it by then swinging their arms as they walked down the path out of the park.

He grumbled out a warning. 'You even think about doing any skipping to go with that arm-swinging and I'm tossing you under the first yellow cab I can find.'

'You're no fun.'

The look he gave her was so heated it practically melted her knees, his voice a low, deliciously sensual rumble. 'Oh, I can be fun. *Believe me.* And now I know how much fun *you* can be, my new aim is to make sure you have as much of it as humanly possible. So consider yourself warned, young lady.'

Kerry grinned the whole way out of the park. She could quite happily have the day never end…

CHAPTER THREE

LITTLE did she know it but Kerry Doyle had managed a bit of a miracle in the twelve hours Ronan had spent with her. She was a ray of sunshine. And, caught in her reflected warmth, he'd miraculously forgotten his reason for being in New York this time round.

It wasn't until the end of the night tour on another open-topped bus that he was faced with a very visible reminder of why he would never be able to forget, because when the light dimmed his world went dark, and he had to force his other senses into overdrive to keep from showing his weakness in front of her.

Thankfully Kerry had been distracted by all the varying photo opportunities afforded to her by the stunning sight of Manhattan lit up against the night sky Ronan didn't have to look at to know—so indelibly was it imprinted onto his mind after dozens of trips. And by the time they'd returned to Times Square he had enough light to work with to leave her with his pride intact.

He frowned as he stepped off the bus, jostling a couple of people in the crowd before he focussed hard on Kerry. He then allowed himself the luxury of studying her face one more time—watching as the newly familiar soft smile formed on her full lips.

Resentment built inside him like a tidal wave. In another

life he wouldn't have been letting her go. He'd have suggested sushi or lobster or cocktails in one of the bars overlooking the free floorshow that was Times Square at night. He'd have taken her back to the Empire State before it closed so she could see the panoramic view of the city from eighty-odd floors up and he'd have walked her back to her hotel—no matter how far it was—and kissed her long and slow before persuading her to spend another day with him.

Though being gentlemanly enough to leave after the kiss might have taken some effort—he had a sneaking suspicion kissing her might be something he didn't want to stop doing in any great hurry.

'Are you hungry?'

Not in the way she probably meant. Looking at her all day had brought on the kind of hunger he hadn't experienced in a long time, if ever. As if she'd uncovered something his body was desperately lacking and now that it knew it craved it as badly as the air he breathed.

He saw the open warmth in her face as the question hung between them and felt momentarily angry at the universe for having to turn her down. 'I've gotta go. I have an early appointment.'

At least he wasn't telling her a lie.

She nodded, turning her face away, then leaning her head back a little to smile up at him one last time, one hand resting on the bag at her hip, the other waving out to her side as she raised her voice enough to be heard over the hundreds upon hundreds of people and honking car horns and the yelled voices of vendors selling everything from fake designer label handbags to T-shirts to hotdogs to—

'I had an amazing day—thank you.'

And there was that word 'amazing' again. Somehow he knew he'd always associate it with her, 'You're welcome. I haven't been on one of those buses for years. But they're a good way to get your bearings the first time. Stick to them and crowds and you won't go too far wrong. No more flirting with strangers, mind.'

She laughed when he added the last part with an edge of mock severity to his voice. 'I'll keep it in mind. And I might take your advice on the helicopter ride before I leave too.'

'You should.'

'Another moment to remember…'

'Exactly.'

He stayed focussed on her and only her for as long as he could manage it without inviting the usual ache behind his eyes, but when it was getting too uncomfortable and he opened his mouth to say the words to let him walk away she distracted him again by moving in to place a warm kiss on his cheek.

It was *her* fault.

Because if she hadn't done it he wouldn't have had the opportunity he now had. He might have resisted the temptation to take one last memory with him, but now he couldn't, turning his head and pressing his mouth to hers before she had time to react. His hand lifted to cradle the back of her head, he took a step in so his body was close enough to hers to feel the added heat in the humid air, and only then did he close his eyes and let his lips drag over hers the way he'd been thinking about doing since he'd met her.

Every hair on his body immediately tingled with awareness; she tasted of the iced coffee they'd stopped for, a hint of raspberry flavouring lingering on her lips and practically begging him to sample more with the tip of his tongue.

So he did. He had to.

For a second Kerry froze, hands floundering on either side of her body while she was caught in the indecision of reaching for him or simply waiting until the world stopped tilting beneath her feet. Oh, heavens above, but the man had sinfully magic lips! And even while alarm bells rang in her head, they were already being drowned out by the sound of her own blood roaring in her ears.

When he ran the tip of his tongue over the parting in her lips, she opened up and met him in the middle, feeling his low hum of approval all the way to the tips of her toes.

When someone bumped her arm, Ronan's arm circled her waist—drawing her in against the protective hard planes of his body as he spread his feet wider. And Kerry's wavering arms automatically lifted in response, her hands settling on his shoulders while she instinctively stood on the balls of her feet to get closer still.

She wasn't even aware of the fact there were other people around them after that. All there was was him and the kissing. *Oh, my, the kissing.* Kerry had honestly thought she'd been kissed before—had she been able to think in a straight line she'd probably have had a look back in her memory to check. But after this—

She sighed contently. It was bliss.

Ronan tilted her back a little so he could kiss her deeper still. And it wasn't a hard kiss, or a kiss that said they were seconds away from being horizontal; in fact it was the very controlled softness and warmth of it, as if he was holding back from her, that wrapped tight around her heart and made it ache for more.

It was a kiss goodbye, wasn't it? He was ending the amazing day with an even more amazing kiss goodbye. And knowing that made Kerry ache as she'd never ached.

His hand slid forwards so that his thumb was brushing against her cheek when he lifted his head, a small frown deepening the crease between his dark brows as he blinked hard to focus on her. While Kerry in turn looked back at him with drowsy, heavy-lidded eyes and somehow eventually managed the energy to smile.

Ronan smiled back a split second before he removed his

hand, loosened his arm and stepped away from her, his voice just husky enough for her to know she wasn't the only one affected by the kiss.

'Enjoy your trip, Kerry, Kerry Doyle.'

She swallowed, smile wavering. 'I'll try.'

There really didn't seem to be much more to say. And she didn't want to ruin the perfect ending to a perfect day by trying to force out words that currently didn't exist in her scrambled brain. So she stepped back, turning her head to get her bearings before deciding to simply flag down a cab and head back to her hotel. After all, anything she did alone would only make her miss his company after everything they'd done together. She missed him already.

When she looked back he was gone and it took a few minutes for her to see his head in the crowd. He obviously wasn't one for long goodbyes, then. What man ever was?

And if she was honest, Kerry didn't think she'd have been able to say it either. So instead she stood still until she couldn't see him any more, only then turning in a circle to look at all the wondrous sights around her. It was a different universe. One city with a larger population than the entire island she lived on.

And she'd just been kissed senseless in the middle of Times Square by a good-looking guy she'd met on a plane less than twenty-four hours ago. How incredible was that?

She laughed, shaking her head at the sheer unexpectedness of it. Kerry Doyle. Kissing what amounted to a stranger in a strange land.

It was the stuff of dreams.

Ronan fiddled with the straw in his glass, rattling ice cubes against the edges while he looked out the large windows beside him and did his best to focus on the odd passer-by in the crowd.

The odd *specific* passer-by, that was…

At first he refused to admit everyone he focussed on was female, with brown hair and so much as the vaguest hint of Kerry to them. But after the sixth or seventh one he eventually told himself it was a natural reaction—an offshoot from numerous daily forays into wondering what she was doing and seeing.

Another brown-haired female walked into his line of vision and he turned his head to follow her, Al's voice sounding from across the table.

'I'm assuming from the fact we're avoiding talking about it that your appointment didn't go so well.'

'We're still not talking about it.'

'Right.'

Frowning when he confirmed it wasn't Kerry and promising himself he wasn't searching for her again, he turned his head to look at his old friend, making sure he was looking him straight in the eye before he spoke with enough of an edge in his voice to hint heavily that he wasn't about to be drawn out.

'Looking to help me drown my sorrows? 'Cos I should warn you I have a curfew these days—so if we're heading out on a pub crawl we need to get started sooner rather than later.'

The last thing he needed was a post-mortem on his appointment with the specialist. It had been a shot in the dark at best—no pun intended. But that didn't mean he wasn't going to try. What it *should* have meant was he wasn't surprised by the negative results.

He supposed he must still have hoped, though…

Al frowned. 'How can you make with the funnies?'

Ronan shrugged. 'How can I not? I'm Irish, Al—you take away my sense of humour, you may as well put me in a box and dig a hole.'

'You're barely thirty-two, Ronan.'

'And I've had my whole life to prepare for this so it's not like it's that big a shock. My uncle has lived with it since he was a kid—so I'm the lucky one.'

With a shake of his head Ronan knew signalled resignation, Al leaned back in his seat and glanced around the sports bar. 'You can't take this trip on your own—not this time.'

'Watch me try.'

'One more book will make that big a difference in the greater scheme of things, will it?'

Ronan shrugged again, leaning forwards and resting his forearms on the table as he watched the ice continue circling in the glass long after he'd finished moving it. 'Will to me.'

'Not like you need the money.'

'Not doing it for the money.'

There was a brief silence and then a low, 'I know.'

Slapping his palms on the wooden surface, Ronan sat upright again. 'Right, then—if you're gonna go all morbid on me I think I prefer you drunk. Let's go.'

'Last time I got drunk with you—'

'I swear—not over the state line this time.'

'Better not be.' Producing his wallet, he checked the bill on the table. 'My wife wasn't happy with a call from Boston that early in the morning.'

'Still came and got us, though.'

'Yeah, and still gives me hell for it. In this country we're s'posed to quit that kinda stupidity once we leave college.'

They pushed their chairs back at the same time, and Ronan stepped over and slapped a hand on Al's back, forcing himself to grin broadly. 'See, you needed me to keep you young. You'll have to find another partner in crime after this—I'll be relying on hearing about your adventures to keep *me* young.'

'Lauren says you'll be eighteen your whole life.'

'From her lips to God's ears, my friend…'

They were almost at the door when for some unknown reason Ronan looked up at the large screen on the wall. It was normally filled with the usual sights of football or baseball or basketball—dependent on the time of year—so he was surprised to catch sight of a news report. And for a second his heart actually stopped.

'What?'

He frowned in concentration, ignoring Al's curious voice as he attempted to read the bulletins across the bottom of the screen—his frustration rising.

'Can someone turn it up?' When it didn't happen immediately, he turned his attention to the people around him, his voice rising. '*Hey!* Turn it up!'

'…to recap…a sightseeing chopper crashed into the Hudson an hour ago…four tourists and the pilot were picked up by—'

Damn it.

Kerry felt she'd been remarkably restrained in the few souvenirs she'd picked up. With the current exchange rate and an array of shops to leave any sane woman drooling, it had taken a gargantuan effort not to shop as if the end of the world were nigh. But she had several thousand miles to go yet and, in fairness, Ronan had been right about her luggage. But then so had she—she *needed* all that stuff.

Could hardly leave New York empty-handed, though…

Smiling brightly at the doorman who'd been her best friend since she checked in, she dropped her chin to look in her bag for her key-card, knowing her way to the elevators well enough not to have to look up again until she had it in her hand.

'Not floating at the bottom of the Hudson, then,' a deep voice rumbled from over her right shoulder.

And Kerry's eyes widened before she swung round, her voice a little breathless in response to the sight of him calmly folding a newspaper and setting it on a coffee-table before he pushed to his feet. *'Ronan.'*

She gulped down a breath, 'How did you—?'

'I have my ways; took a couple of hours and a friend on a second phone, mind you. I take it you skipped my advice about a helicopter ride on your last day.'

She blinked at him. 'I was going to take one but—'

'You heard one fell in the river?'

'Yeah, well, that kinda thing can be a little off-putting even when nobody got hurt so—' It suddenly hit her why he might be there, her mouth curling into a smile in response. 'You were worried about me?'

His stunning eyes narrowed a little as he got closer, large hands casually pushing back the edges of his tan linen jacket so he could shove them down into the pockets of his light-coloured chinos.

'Thought I'd check—that's all.'

It was quite possibly the sweetest thing any man had ever done for her. But when how she felt must have shown in her eyes he frowned, shaking his head and drawing his mouth into a thin line before he got to her. 'Having advised you to go I might have felt guilty if you'd ended up getting wet again so—'

'Thank you.'

She smiled all the more when he looked irritated. Well, he'd just have to learn to accept the consequences of being sweet if he took it on himself to be that way. Though somehow she doubted he was the kind of man who'd appreciate being *told* he was sweet in the first place.

There were other things she could tell him she thought he was, mind you…

He dropped his chin and looked down at her bags, sinfully gorgeous lips twitching when he looked back into her eyes.

'You didn't seriously go out and buy more stuff to cart around on your trip?'

Kerry lifted her chin. 'A couple of souvenirs.'

'Uh-huh—and they needed that many bags, did they?'

'And a couple of things for friends…'

'Which you're *posting* home, I assume?'

Actually that wasn't a half-bad idea. If she'd thought of that she could have bought more. Maybe if she went back she could—

A hand appeared to wave a forefinger at her. 'Oh, no, you don't. You buy this much stuff at every destination, you're going to need a packhorse before long. Remember we talked about *downsizing*?'

'Have I just been adopted?'

The smile he gave her was disgustingly sensual, and mesmerizing as all hell. He even dropped his voice an octave so the air between them vibrated. 'Maybe.'

Kerry blinked at him again, lost for words, and, as she had spent almost half her life talking to people from all walks of life, it was quite an event.

He nodded once at the bags. 'Do you need to leave those up to your room?'

'Why? Where am I going?'

'You're bound to be hungry after all that shopping.'

'Maybe I already ate.'

'Did you?'

'No.' And yes, she could have lied about that, but she'd never been much good at lying. Do unto others and all that, she'd always reckoned. 'But maybe I don't want to eat *with you* now you're exhibiting these new stalker-like tendencies.'

'Yes, you do.' He rocked forwards onto the balls of his feet and quirked dark brows at her, light dancing in his eyes. 'And now I've adopted you it's my responsibility to make sure you're fed and watered.'

Kerry's eye's narrowed.

And Ronan chuckled as he rocked back onto his heels. 'And, anyway, I've been doing some thinking while I sat here waiting to make sure you hadn't drowned and I might have a proposition to put to you…'

The words dangled in the air between them like a flipping carrot, just enough of a mystery to pique her interest all over again. 'What kind of "proposition"?'

'Come to dinner and I'll consider telling you.'

'What does it say in your handbook about women travelling alone accepting random dinner invitations from men seeking to proposition them?'

'That might just be part of it.'

If it turned out Ronan was indeed a serial killer Kerry vowed she was haunting her nana in retaliation for all the Hardy Boys and Nancy Drew books she'd been given as a child, feeding her a love of mystery from an impressionable age. And she silently prayed she hadn't chosen this particular moment to be completely wrong about someone.

'Do I need to get changed?'

The question gave him an open invitation to look down over her body, which he did—at length—doing that weird skipping thing to her pulse rate he was so very good at.

When his gaze eventually tangled with hers again the darker blue was distinctly more prominent than any of the other shades. 'You'll do.'

Kerry damped her lips, waving a handful of shopping bags in the direction of the front doors. 'Well, go on, then. I'll leave my bags with the doorman. But my flight's tomorrow so we can't be out too late.'

Warm fingers wrapped around her elbow as he guided her to the door. 'We'll be back well before either of us turn into pumpkins.'

Dinner, naturally, had to be yet another experience she'd

remember. And leaning back in her seat, a large bowled glass of rich Cabernet Shiraz in hand and her stomach ridiculously full of the kind of pasta that had simply melted in her mouth, Kerry couldn't help but smile at her surroundings. Trust Ronan.

Little Italy was packed—the one narrow street made even narrower by all the tables full of diners spilling out from a cornucopia of small restaurants. And then there were all the people milling around trying to decide where to eat, and the sound of laughter and voices yelling out greeting and music spilling out to compete with music from further down the street. It was gloriously insane. Kerry *loved* it.

The world was a wonderful place with a little of his perspective.

Ronan leaned forwards, frowning the way he always did when he was studying her intently. 'Dessert?'

Kerry laughed. 'Are you kidding me? Those portions were big enough for three people—though I appreciate your restraint at eating the courses in the right order for a change.'

'So you should. And there's always room for dessert—trust me.'

She watched as he absent-mindedly rolled the sleeves of his crisp white shirt a little higher up his forearms, her gaze captivated by the movement of his long fingers. Then she looked up and watched as he turned his head to look into the crowd, thick lashes brushing against his skin as he blinked.

Somehow she doubted watching him would ever get boring—he was constantly studying his surroundings, taking everything in and most likely making mental notes, his obvious intelligence just adding to his attractiveness and making her burn to know how his mind worked. The suspense was killing her.

'Okay, now I'm fed and watered—out with it.'

She saw him shake his head before he turned to face her, tutting. '*Before* coffee?'

Kerry giggled, her eyes widening in surprise at the sound before she set her glass firmly away from her. That was quite enough of that stuff, then.

'The suspense is killing me. So spill it.'

'Three days in the States and she's already picking up the lingo.'

When she threw a warning glare his way he smiled lazily, leaning forward to rest his elbows on the table, long fingers playing with the cutlery he hadn't used while he studied her face. And under the influence of the sense-numbing wine it took a moment for her brain to kick in with a possible motive for his stalling.

'Whatever it is you're not entirely convinced it's that good an idea, are you?'

Ronan's brows jerked. 'And how exactly would you know that?'

Kerry waved a limp hand back and forth in front of her. 'Female intuition. We're born with it.'

He nodded at the table. 'How many glasses of that have we had, young lady?'

'Not enough to lose my ability to think. So if you don't think it's that good an idea why are you about to suggest it?'

His chest rose and fell. 'Good question.'

'Well, don't suggest it, then, if you're so unconvinced.' She reached for her glass, hiding her nose in it and her eyes from his intense gaze while she swallowed her sudden sense of disappointment with another mouthful of rich liquid.

'I want to suggest it even more now you've said that—if it was a go at reverse psychology then *bravo…*'

Kerry pursed her lips at the tinge of sarcasm, nodding firmly while focussing her attention on swirling what was left in her glass round and round in circles. 'It wasn't. But if that's how you feel then you definitely *should* suggest it. Go with your gut, shoot from the hip, live life without regrets, fortune favours the—'

She had dozens of these. But Ronan caught her attention by waving his arm at a waiter, smiling while he raised his voice to be heard above the background noise.

'Tiramisu and two coffees, please—the lady will have hers black.'

Kerry scowled at him.

And he chuckled throatily in reply, eyes still twinkling with amusement when he then leaned over the table, lifting a hand to beckon her with the same forefinger he'd waggled earlier.

'Come here, crazy girl.'

With a very deep breath Kerry fought the urge to be petulant and leaned forwards, setting her glass down on the white tablecloth and resting her elbows the same way Ronan had. Then she simply quirked her brows in silent question, and waited.

He examined her eyes for the longest time, as if sizing her up before he made his decision. 'What age are you Kerry, Kerry Doyle?'

What did that have to do with anything?

'Why? Do you want to add old to drunk and crazy?'

'No—and I don't think you're drunk; just slightly sozzled. You're obviously not much of a drinker—' he smiled a smile that warmed her inside more than the wine had, his voice dropping seductively '—but I'm sticking with the crazy.'

Actually she was nearly as okay with that as she'd been with him thinking she was beautiful. Crazy was much more interesting than the sensible or practical or reliable tags normally associated with her name.

'Why do you need to know what age I am?'

His eyes narrowed an almost imperceptible amount, the gaze so intense she could feel her toes curling. 'You're currently a bit of a conundrum, that's why.'

Her eyes widened in surprise. 'I am?'

'Answer the question.'

Kerry sighed dramatically, mumbling beneath her breath, 'Thirty-six.'

'Didn't quite catch that.'

So she reluctantly raised her voice. 'Thirty-six, *okay*? Now tell me why you needed to know so badly you broke the "never ask a lady her age" rule.'

'Right up there with the dessert rule, is it?'

'*Higher.*'

Amusement shone in his eyes, even while he shook his head. 'You don't look thirty-six.'

'Thanks. I think. Now what does my age have to do with your proposition?' On top of the effects of half a glass of wine too many, her head was starting to ache attempting to figure him out. So if blunt was what it was going to take…

The nod was barely perceptible, but enough when accompanied with another intense gaze for her to know that whatever doubt he'd had about what he was going to suggest was now gone.

'I've had an idea for a new book. And I want to hire you to help me research it—with mutually beneficial perks along the way.'

'Mutually beneficial *how*, exactly?'

'*That* we'll discuss over coffee…'

CHAPTER FOUR

'I NEED that one.'

'Why do you need it?'

Kerry snatched the dress out of his hands and put it on the 'keeper' pile. 'Because it's the only long evening dress I have with me.'

Ronan lifted it back out and tossed it on the other pile on top of her bed. 'Unless you're planning on attending an embassy ball in one of the countries we visit—you don't need it.' He sighed with exasperation, 'Woman—exactly *how many* pairs of shoes do you have with you?'

Rescuing the sandals, she held them behind her back and lifted her chin to defy him. 'The shoes *stay*.'

'All thirty pairs of them? You only have *two* feet. Who are you—Imelda Marcos?'

She made the mistake of bringing the sandals out to wave them at him. 'These are *comfortable*.'

He grabbed them. 'They're exactly the same as the pair I already let you have.'

'No, they're not—these are *white*.' She held onto them as if her life depended on it.

He smiled lazily and she hated him for it. Hadn't she already compromised enough by letting him take over every-thing to begin with—changing her schedule left, right and centre so he could take her to what he considered to be the best places to see? Not that she hadn't enjoyed every single second of the nine-day Whistler Mountaineer tour they'd taken through the Canadian Rockies, something she'd probably never have thought of doing—mainly because she hadn't actually known about it, but still…

What the time had done was demonstrate the change in their relationship—they had moved from personal to almost professional. Yes, his proposition to act as travel guide while recording her reactions along the way had done that to begin with—but the first leg of their trip had highlighted it in spades. And, honestly, she kinda missed the ease they'd had with each other in New York. Her luggage was almost the last straw.

He tugged. 'Which just makes them more of a candidate for the reject pile. White isn't practical.'

Kerry, the queen of practicality under normal circumstances, tugged right on back.

'White goes with everything.'

'That's what you said about the same pair in the pale beige colour.'

'*Nude.*' When his eyes sparkled dangerously she felt an unwanted wave of heat building on her neck, gritting her teeth to add, 'The *colour* is called "nude".'

Humming under his breath, Ronan leaned his face a little closer to hers. 'For a second there I thought you were making a suggestion.'

He'd said it on such a low, flat tone that she wasn't sure if he was flirting or not.

'You should be so lucky.' Having mumbled back her reply, she decided the best way out of her current predicament might be to negotiate, especially since his proximity was distracting her so badly from her goal. Even after ten days in each other's company practically 24/7 he still had that effect on her.

And they hadn't kissed again or come anywhere close to it, but it certainly hadn't stopped her from thinking about it every single time she looked at him.

'I'll trade you.'

Letting go of the shoes, he held both hands up in surrender. 'Shoes for a little nudity? You're on.'

Kerry rolled her eyes. 'You're still completely incorrigible.'

Lowering his arms, he folded them across his broad chest and came back with, 'Yes, but you know that after this long. I have to say, though—you must really love those shoes.'

'I wasn't actually offering any nudity.'

'Spoilsport. So what is it you're offering in exchange? 'Cos everything in this pile is going; dragging around all that luggage is tiring me out.'

'You aren't the one dragging it round!'

'True, but watching you struggle with it is tiring.'

'You could have offered to help.'

'And how exactly would I prove my point that way?'

Kerry growled at him and Ronan had to use every ounce of his self-control not to laugh out loud. In fairness, she'd been a good sport about everything so far—for the most part. Though when he'd ripped up her colour-coded schedule in front of her she had gone a little pale. And that was after her jaw had dropped when he'd decided to shake up the majority of her flights and cancel all her hotel reservations.

But if this 'spur of the moment' idea of his was going to work all the way round the planet, then she had to trust him. And she'd loved the train trip, hadn't she? Every single day greeted with the kind of enthusiasm that had made him remember all over again how he'd felt when he'd first taken up travelling himself.

Which would have been a nice reminder if it hadn't stung a little—but, much as it galled him, Al had been right: there was no way realistically he could take a chance the whole way round the world on his own this time—Kerry was backup. He'd rot in hell before he was forced to tell her that, though, or why; most of all *why*.

He watched as she thought over her next move, smiling inwardly at the amount of effort she felt she had to put into negotiating with him. She over-thought things in his opinion—the caution at odds with the unfettered enthusiasm she'd displayed for everything they'd done so far. And he hadn't even got started yet…

'I'll trade three items for three questions.'

Her eyes narrowed. 'What kind of questions?'

'Questions like the kind you've been neatly sidestepping ever since you agreed to this.' He nodded when she avoided his gaze, 'Yes, I had noticed. I'm observant that way. It's starting to feel like I'm travelling with an international spy—well, one that's never been anywhere that is…'

'And this is part of your research for *The Virgin Traveller*, is it?'

'That's still a working title and, no, it's because I have a few things I still don't get about you.'

Kerry wrapped her arms around her midriff, shoes dangling off her thumbs. And Ronan recognized the move as a defensive one before she asked; 'Like what, for instance?'

He had a bit of a list, as it happened, but he figured it might be best to start with something simple. 'Like why you've waited this long to visit all the places you've dreamed of seeing, *for instance*—was money a problem?'

The frown was immediate, and she avoided his gaze again—so much for something simple. Except now he wanted to know all the more.

'If I know you better I can tailor the trip better.'

'You were doing fine until the luggage issue.'

The fact she mumbled her reply again had him fighting off yet another smile. She had an uncanny knack for doing that, as if she could reach an invisible hand inside his chest and tug the smile out of him. 'You'll thank me later.'

'You'll see I'm right to complain when I have to make you go *shopping* later.'

Wasn't ever gonna happen—he'd made the mistake of shopping with a woman once in his adult life and had taken a solemn vow it would never happen again. They made it into some weird test of a man's patience.

'I'll even let shoes be one item when technically they're two.'

'That's big of you.'

It was going to take a little more persuasion, wasn't it? He could be persuasive if that was what it took. And at least when he stepped closer it got her to look up into his eyes again—so he unfolded his arms to make more room in case he needed to get closer still. It didn't take a lot of encouragement, as it happened, not when he'd been fighting the idea of getting closer for ten days solid. He knew it was a *bad idea* though…

'You can't keep lugging those cases everywhere.' He let a slow smile loose on her, watching as her gaze dropped briefly to his mouth and then back up, the simple action intensely provocative, if unintentionally. 'You have to trust me.'

The tip of her tongue swept across her lips, drawing his gaze down the same way she'd just done with him. 'I do trust you. I wouldn't be here if I didn't.'

It happened on its own; almost instinctively his hands lifted to her upper arms, fingertips sliding up and down her baby-soft skin to soothe her. Having her stuff with her was a kind of security blanket; he got that. Especially knowing how much she liked itineraries and organization and being prepared for every eventuality. And the fact she trusted him meant something to him, his voice lowering in reaction.

'Your female intuition says I'm a good guy, does it?'

Kerry smiled a small smile, goose-bumps appearing on her

skin beneath his fingers, her voice equally as low as his. 'Don't think I don't know what you're doing…'

A part of his subconscious mind turned his hands over so he was running the backs of his fingers over her skin, searing heat tingling over his knuckles, up his wrists and into his forearms while he breathed deep breaths of her fresh flower scent and took a step closer until his toes were touching hers,

'What am I doing?'

She damped her lips again and Ronan couldn't help but wonder if she had any idea how big an invitation it was. She was a grown woman, after all, so how could she not know? But he'd promised himself he wouldn't take advantage of her on this trip. It was pointless after all and it'd been the only thing to persuade him it might work—for both of them.

The husky edge to her voice didn't help any. 'You're doing that thing you do when you know you need to up the ante to bend me to your will. You don't travel with other people much, do you? You're used to taking charge and doing things your own way.'

He quirked his brows. *'Bend you to my will?'*

She shrugged, frowning at a point at the base of his throat. 'Get your own way, then—win—whatever phraseology you want to use.'

'Yes, because you make winning so easy for me.'

Her gaze rose. 'It's the very fact I don't that makes you use this tactic, though, isn't it? You think it's your trump card. I voice a doubt or dig my heels in or ask about your plans and you turn on the charm to distract me.'

'Not working this time, I take it?'

A burst of almost nervous laughter brought the smile back to his face, and Kerry's chin came up another notch in return. 'I'm immune to this tactic now.'

Oh, was she indeed?

If something didn't stop him soon there was a very good

chance that promise of his was about to get broken—or at least adjusted some to suit the situation.

'I need to up my game, then, do I?'

'You can't kiss me into submission, Ronan.'

'And now she's challenging me…'

She started backing away, her eyes wide with surprise and glittering with awareness. 'When you sold this trip to me you didn't mention anything about random kissing being part of the deal.'

'You didn't complain in Times Square.'

'That was different.'

'Different how?'

Her mouth opened, then closed, then opened again. A dangling shoe was waved at him. And she was still backing away. 'That was a spur-of-the-moment kiss—a "perfect end to a perfect day kiss"—a "we know we'll never see each other again so it doesn't really matter" kiss. Whereas this, this—well, this is—'

'Different?'

'It's you attempting to kiss me to the point where I won't be able to think—like last time—only this time—' Her cheeks turned the most endearing shade of pink at the confession and Ronan found himself smiling all the more as he stalked her across the room.

He liked when she blushed.

She damped her lips one more time before continuing, the shoe waving in warning. 'You're playing dirty.'

And yet the sparkling in her eyes and the smile twitching at the corners of her mouth indicated she was quite enjoying that he was playing dirty. Even without the confession that he could kiss her to the point of not being able to think.

He liked that he'd been able to do that.

'I did say I'd trade questions for shoes, but you turned that down.'

'You said items—not shoes specifically.'

'Yes, but you've fought more over shoes than anything else.'

She backed herself into an armchair—literally. Because when the backs of her knees hit it, she flopped downwards, losing a shoe over one edge in the process. And when she immediately twisted round, scrambling to get it before he could, he took one long stride forwards, bent over at the waist and dropped his hands onto the rolled arms so she was trapped.

The triumphant smile she'd worn as she twisted back up with the shoe safely in hand faded when she realized her mistake. But she didn't lean back into the deep upholstery; instead she tilted her head back and her wide-eyed gaze tangled with his.

Man, but she was beautiful.

He spread his feet wide, bending at the knees so he could lean his upper body lower still, his voice dropping to the intimate level they'd got so good at using when they talked on a plane.

'And just think…'

A shrill ringing sounded from near the open suitcases, forcing Ronan to look over his shoulder to try and locate where it was coming from.

'It's my mobile.' Kerry poked him in the chest with her shoes. 'I've got to answer it—it'll be from home. I promised I'd check in at regular intervals.'

Saved by the bell. Probably just as well too.

'Very sensible—we can put that in the book.'

Kerry held her breath for the brief amount of time it took for him to make the decision to push upright and walk to the phone, only letting it out when she allowed herself to admit she was disappointed he had.

She'd *wanted* him to kiss her again *darn it*! What did a girl have to do—throw herself at him? And he had no one to blame but himself. If that first kiss hadn't been so—*memorable*, she mightn't feel the need to find out if she'd built it up out of all proportion in her head...

But it wasn't as if he'd shown any inclination to repeat it, was it? Not 'til now, anyway. And it probably wasn't a good idea—not while they were travelling together. If it fell apart, then that would be the end of the trip, and if it got serious it wasn't as if he were the kind of man who would settle down in a nine-to-five.

Didn't stop her from aching for the loss of a kiss that never happened, though, did it? Oh, no.

When he tossed her phone across the room she dropped her shoes, cupping her hands to neatly catch it before smirking triumphantly at him because she had and hitting the answer key.

'Hello?'

'Where in hell are you?'

'Yes, lovely to hear from you too—I'm in San Francisco.' She bent over at the waist to retrieve a shoe that had slid off her lap onto the floor between her feet, effectively hiding the frown on her face caused by her cousin's tone. 'I emailed you about the change of plans, remember?'

'You're travelling with a complete stranger you met on a plane? Have you lost your mind?'

'He's not a professional kidnapper, Ellie.'

Ronan's deep voice grumbled from across the room, 'If I was I'd have got rid of this luggage sooner.'

Kerry glared at him when he lifted his chin to look at her, her eyes narrowing when she heard a zipper being pulled and she realized what he was doing. 'You go anywhere near my underwear and you're a dead man.'

The thought of him lifting out the frivolous items one by one and deciding what she should and shouldn't wear was enough to form the suggestion of a low moan in the base of her throat. One that was accompanied with a sudden rush of warmth all over her body—

'*What?*'

The shriek in her ear made her grimace. 'Nothing. I wasn't talking to you.'

'He's there now?'

'Yes, he's persuading me to downsize my luggage.'

'In your *room*?'

Kerry couldn't help but smile at the Victorian sense of outrage. With her younger cousin's chequered history in the affair department it wasn't as if she really had the right to throw any stones, was it?

'Yes, in my room. He's attempting to get a sneak peak at my underwear while you're distracting me.'

There was a distinct silence on the other end of the line while Ronan's mouth quirked, at least three items she was going to debate later being tossed on the rapidly growing 'discarded' pile. And that very hint of amusement told her the thought of the underwear had indeed crossed his mind. He really was a bit of a devil.

But it was part of his attraction. That and the way he looked and that incorrigible streak of his. Was it any wonder she was so obsessed with the idea of more kissing?

'You're sharing a room with this guy?'

She rolled her eyes at the recriminating tone. 'No, he has his own room—not that it would be any of your business if he didn't.'

'*Kerry!*'

'Ellie, don't, c'mon, have you ever known me to do anything spectacularly stupid?'

There was only a brief pause this time. 'No. That's why this is worrying everyone so much. You know the family was never happy with the idea of you taking this trip on your own.'

'I'm not on my own any more, am I?'

'But we don't know anything about this guy.'

'I'm getting a little too long in the tooth for you lot to decide who I can and can't spend time with, don't you think? You were all going to fight me on this trip regardless.' She frowned a little when Ronan's dark brows lifted.

He'd just got a little insight on her life with his eavesdropping, hadn't he?

'So we're not supposed to care now?'

Oh, for crying out loud!

She sighed heavily, 'I didn't say that.'

'What would happen to the hotel if something happened to you?'

Yes, because everything in the Doyle family life revolved around the hotel, didn't it? But, having already given up so much for it, Kerry really didn't feel three months was that much to ask for.

'Did something happen at the hotel?'

'No. Not yet anyway. But Doyle's isn't—'

'Doyle's without a Doyle at the helm—yes, I know the mantra, thanks.' She pushed to her feet and began pacing the way she normally did at home. 'But if it can't survive three months without me after fifteen years of making sure it runs like a well-oiled machine, then I haven't done much of a job, have I? Did Dad make you call me?'

'Well, when I told him about the email—'

'I thought so. Well, I'm not coming home early and you can just tell him that. If he wants a Doyle at Doyle's he can come out of retirement and do it himself.' And if she'd thought for a single second he would she'd have been on the first plane home. But he knew what she'd do if he tried to change what she'd done to the place. Complete autonomy was the one thing she'd insisted on when she'd given up every dream of her own.

Kerry swore silently as the all-too-familiar headache

rolled in over her temples, glancing at Ronan from the corner of her eye to see what he was doing. She didn't doubt for a second he was still listening—but what she wasn't prepared for was the sight of him holding up a nightdress he'd found, dangling the item in front of him from shoestring straps hooked off his thumbs.

His gaze rose and tangled with hers. And Kerry had to swallow hard when it felt as if a bolt of pure electricity shot across the room. Suddenly she couldn't seem to breathe, and her stomach did a weird kind of flip-flop thing.

She damped her lips. He blinked slowly a few times. And then it went on the 'keeper' pile before he dropped his chin and went back to work…

Oh, my.

Her cousin brought her back to earth with a bump. 'I don't think it'll come to that, Kerry, but he *is* worried about you. And Nana—'

'Oh-h-h—' Kerry laughed sarcastically, '—don't you dare tell me Nana told you to check up on me. Nana would be more interested in what Ronan looks like than she would about him being a possible kidnapper. In fact she'd find that an interesting facet to his personality. She's the only one who was behind me on this trip to begin with—it's the trip she'd have taken herself if—'

She *really* needed to get her cousin off the phone before her entire family history was hauled unceremoniously out of the closet, albeit across the Atlantic via mobile phone. She should just have agreed to the stupid questions-for-items deal—because if he'd wanted personal information, then by now she'd have at least half her stuff back.

She breathed deep, forcing the soothing tone into her voice that always worked best on her highly strung cousin. 'Ellie, I'm *fine*. And I'll be back when I said I'd be back. I promise.'

'At least tell me where you're going to be for the next check-in.' The pout was positively audible.

And it was a good question. One that involved Kerry stopping pacing long enough to look at Ronan again. Where he was merrily tossing item after item onto the discarded pile...

He was frowning and shaking his head at her ceramic straighteners when she asked the question, 'Where are we going to be this time next week?'

His chin lifted, straighteners pointing at his wide chest. 'You asking me?'

'Yes, I'm asking you—you're the one with the itinerary now.'

When he shrugged she dearly wanted to strangle him— because her cousin would be relaying every second of their conversation to Kerry's father within milliseconds of hanging up the phone. And she'd embellish the fact Kerry hadn't a clue where she was going to the extent where it would seem to the entire Doyle clan that she genuinely *had* been kidnapped.

'Fiji.'

'Really?' She couldn't help the bubble of excitement that leapt up into her chest and burst into a full-blown smile on her face.

Another shrug. 'Probably.'

'Ellie, we'll be in—'

'Might still be in Hawaii, though—depends on the flights from Honolulu to Nadi.'

Either one sounded pretty good to her, even with his blasé way of delivering the information as if they were about to run down the street to the corner shop. Yes, Hawaii had been on her original itinerary, but Fiji had been left out. And for the life of her, feeling as excited as she suddenly did at the prospect of going there, she had absolutely no idea why it had.

'Either Hawaii or Fiji—dependent on available flights. So I'll find a way of emailing or calling, even if it's just from the airport.'

'Fiji—seriously?' The jealous tone to Ellie's voice only added to Kerry's change of mood.

'I know!' If she'd been fifteen years younger she'd have jumped up and down.

There was a heartfelt sigh. 'Damn it. He's good-looking too, isn't he?'

'You have no idea.'

CHAPTER FIVE

'So Kerry, Kerry Doyle…'

Kerry was still smiling as she looked out of the windows of the restaurant to the city below, mentally cataloguing all her collected 'moments' from the last two days. From the second they'd made an atmospheric trip across the Golden Gate Bridge, plunging in and out of sunshine and rolling fog, she'd known San Francisco was definitely going on her list of places to come back to. The sun that never seemed to stop shining, the buildings oh-so-white in the bright light, the streets that ran in effortless roller-coasters across the city's many crests and bluffs, sparkling water and monumental bridges more or less permanently in view.

It was wonderful. And that was before she added in the people, who always seemed to end every answer to a question with the word 'enjoy'—which she definitely had. She wasn't quite doing what the song said, but she was leaving *some* of her heart behind.

Ronan was leaning back in his chair when she looked at him, a quiet certainty written across his face. 'You're a Doyle as in "Doyle's of Dublin", aren't you?'

Yep, there it was—though in fairness he'd done well to let it be for as long as he had. But there'd been just enough questions scattered throughout the last forty-eight hours for her to know it was coming, so she wasn't overly surprised.

She took a deep breath, focussing her attention on adding cream to her coffee. *Cream.* Not milk. She'd learnt that from her time in the States—though what that meant they called actual cream, she wasn't quite sure of just yet. They should maybe add some kind of dictionary for the basic necessities in each country to the back of Ronan's new book. She should suggest that—after all, that was why he was playing tour guide for her…

'I hope you're not about to tell me you gave the hotel a bad write-up at some point. I thought we'd been getting on pretty well 'til now—barring the luggage incident that is…'

'Never been.'

'That's almost as bad, coming from a travel expert.'

His sinful mouth quirked. 'It's probably got more to do with the fact I've only ever done an "off the wall" perspective on Dublin. Doyle's is as much of an icon as The Waldorf or The Ritz.'

Kerry inclined her head as she lifted her coffee. 'We like to think so.'

'And you run it.'

'Yes.' She took another deep breath before sipping some of the deliciously bitter blend, a sense of disappointment rising inside her at having to fess up to who she was. It would be a downward slide after that, wouldn't it? The new and improved Kerry she liked so much would once again be placed back into her Doyle wrapping and she'd have to stop pretending she was someone she wasn't.

And she hated letting her go.

When she glanced up from beneath her lashes he had his head to one side, elbows resting on the arms of his chair and his long fingers forming a tent.

'Now I'm even more curious about why you've never taken this trip before—not a money issue, was it?'

Her cup placed carefully back on its saucer without so much as a rattle, she lifted her chin to reply with a calm, 'I'd

have thought it was more obvious why. Running Doyle's is a
big responsibility.'

Ronan nodded his head just the once as he leaned forwards,
lifting his elbows to the table the way he always did and
lowering his tented fingers to the crisp white tablecloth before
continuing with a gentle voice that crept in round the edges
of her heart, 'Don't get defensive on me—there's no need.'

It took a giant effort not to groan, because there was *every*
need. She wanted to be carefree Kerry, she wanted to be
adventurous Kerry, she wanted to be the have-fun Kerry she'd
been with him in New York and during their time in San
Francisco. She wanted to be able to flirt back with him when
he flirted with her—because sometimes he forgot himself,
didn't he? And if they delved into her life she'd have to lose
several of those things. Not least of all because she'd be
reminded once again that getting involved with someone like
him was pointless. Flirting was *bad*.

Stalling the inevitable, she looked back out the window,
shrugging. 'I'm not.'

'Yes, you are.' Warm fingers captured hers on the cloth,
lifting and tangling before squeezing to get her attention.
'And you were different on the phone to home too—your
tone changed, you paced. Bit of a danger of executive stress
in your life, is there?'

Kerry focussed her attention on their joined hands, the
golden glow her skin was acquiring still a great contrast to the
deeper tan on his skin. And then there were the other differences in their hands: his fingers longer and broader with
neatly cut square nails—hers finer boned with the rounded
fingernails painted a pale pink. His hand distinctly male with
a faint smattering of hair bleached almost invisible by the sun
running up onto his forearms from his wrists—her hand small
against his, distinctly feminine...

'You haven't met my cousin—she can *be* stressful.'

'No, I haven't, but Nana sounds like fun.'

Kerry smiled, her gaze flickering over to meet his. 'She is. And she'd love every single second of this trip. In a different age she'd have been one of those intrepid women explorers who tramped across the desert or flew single-handed across oceans.'

The smile she got in reply was so warm she could practically feel her bones softening.

'Well, then, we know where you get your sense of adventure from, don't we?'

Which made her laugh ruefully. 'Oh, you really don't know me at all, do you?'

'Maybe not.' He squeezed her fingers again, waiting for her to look into his eyes before he continued in the low, rumbling tone that always did things for her. 'But you set out to travel around the globe on your own and you agreed to a magical mystery tour with a handsome stranger—that sounds pretty adventurous to me.'

'And yet I still looked so helpless when you met me you felt the need to take me under your wing…'

'Nah.' His stunning eyes sparkled across at her. 'I'm just using you for research purposes.'

When he let his fingers slide free Kerry curled hers into her palm, almost as if she subliminally felt the need to hold onto his warmth. But she smiled in reply.

'At least I know where I stand.'

Ronan's attention turned to his coffee and for no reason Kerry's mind returned to earlier in the day; they'd stopped for more Italian food in the North Beach area of the city, where apparently every Saturday afternoon the restaurant owner and his family would sing opera amongst tile-topped tables like the one they'd been sitting at beneath pictures of 'Papa' posing with Pavarotti.

Both Kerry and Ronan had smiled through the performance of the man who'd told them, 'This place is my life, my music.

I am tenor. My wife is soprano. Is beautiful here. People say: "Papa, don' change." I say: "Don' worry. I won' change."'

But in the middle of the magical singing, Kerry had looked across at Ronan and watched him 'zone out', his thoughts a thousand miles away. He'd frowned, his jaw had clenched, and Kerry had suddenly wondered what it was that was wrong. But then he'd looked at her and smiled one of his slow, disgustingly sexy smiles and she'd found herself smiling back—still burning with the need to know what he'd been thinking.

Looking back, she wondered if it had been that building frustration or the sheer emotion of the singing that made her well up…

Over linguini and clams he'd teased her about being carried away by the romance of the music—typical woman. And she'd parried back that he had no sense of what romance was—typical man.

It had brushed it over, but she still burned to know what he was thinking—even now while he was staring pensively into his coffee—which was probably why she'd remembered what had happened earlier.

But before she could make an attempt at turning the topic of conversation onto him, he lifted the cup and calmly continued with his own line of questioning.

'You've been running the hotel for sixteen years?'

'Fifteen. I was "in training" for the first three until my father had to retire after a heart attack—didn't have a clue what I was doing at the start.'

Ronan's brows lifted in interest. 'Not being groomed from the minute you stepped out of nappies?'

She smiled, despite being forced to look back. 'No—I was never aiming for the family business. It was my brother who spent every spare hour learning the ropes. He even took time doing everyone's job so he could understand what they all did. I thought he was insane.'

'What did you want to do?'

'Ah-h-h…' She grinned. 'I was going to be an artist and live a *very* bohemian lifestyle. The thought of it made my father want to tear his hair out and that only made me want it ten times more in my rebellious teens.'

Ronan's eyes glowed at her, his mouth curling upwards again—most likely in amusement at the idea of her being anywhere vaguely in the region of 'bohemian'. His voice was tinged with a seductive gruffness that sent her pulse fluttering as he asked, 'What kind of artist?'

'A painter—watercolour mostly. I used to be reasonably all right at it too, or so my tutors told me at art college,' She shrugged her shoulders, glancing down as she turned her coffee-cup in circles on the saucer. 'We all have dreams when we're young. But then we grow up and we do what we have to do.'

'What happened?'

She didn't look up as she said the words on a flat tone. 'My brother died.'

When Ronan didn't say anything she made the mistake of looking up, only to find him frowning at her before he asked in the same gruff tone, 'Were you close?'

Kerry smiled wistfully. 'About as close as you can get, I guess. We were twins—a ten-minute gap made me the baby of the family. They run in the family.'

'I'm sorry.'

'Don't be.' She smiled a larger smile to let him know it was okay. 'It was a long time ago. You weren't driving the lorry that hit them. And even if you were I wouldn't for a single second think you killed them on purpose.'

'Them?'

'He was bringing Mum home from the hotel.'

He visibly flinched and, although Kerry appreciated that he understood it had been rough for the family and for her, she'd had time to adjust to it. 'So I stepped into Jamie's shoes, not that I stood much of a chance of filling them when we were so very different. But Doyle's isn't Doyle's without—'

'A Doyle at the helm. Yeah, I heard that part.' He leaned forward in his chair again. 'Different what way?'

'You want my entire life story at one sitting?'

'Well, it's not like you've been willing to share voluntarily up 'til now, is it?'

'I could toss that one right back at you.' Had it possibly been part of the awkwardness she'd felt between them since New York? Two people spending practically 24/7 together could hardly go the guts of three months without getting to know each other better.

'I got here first.' His fingertips toyed with hers on the table-cloth again, thick lashes lowering and a small frown reappearing on his face, as if he hadn't even realized he'd reached for her until he felt her skin. 'Different how?'

'Nope, your turn—you always want to be a travel writer? You have brothers or sisters? Mum and Dad still around? Come on—fair's fair.'

'Always wanted to travel.' He shrugged. 'Writing about it was a natural progression. Two sisters—both married and I'm an uncle three and half times…'

She laughed, enchanted by the deep affection in his voice. 'How can you be half an uncle, you idiot?'

Leaning even further forwards, he brought his other hand into play, turning hers over and cradling it while he traced her palm with his forefinger. 'It's not due 'til Christmas.'

'Ah.' It was the only response she could manage while he was doing what he was doing to her hand.

'I've put in my request for another girl—I'm three for three so far.' Another small frown accompanied his words.

'Girls tend to hero-worship their Indiana-Jones-type uncles, do they?'

'Something like that.' He looked up from her hand long

enough to flash a devilish sparkle-eyed smile. 'I should get the hat, really, shouldn't I?'

'We can look out for one on our travels.'

'Wouldn't that involve shopping?'

'I've been really good so far.'

'You have. But don't think I'm not watching you every second. Just 'cos we posted home that parcel of unnecessary accoutrements doesn't mean you get to race out and replace them all.'

Kerry rolled her eyes. 'This is going to be the longest trip in the history of circumnavigation if I can't shop so much as once. You're stomping on my fantasy list a little, you know.'

His fingertip kept tracing lazy circles on her overly sensitive palm, the touch more erotic than anything she'd ever experienced. Oh, Lord, would he take so much time touching everywhere? Would he look at her the way he was right that second while he did? All heat and intensity and radiating toe-curling sensuality…

Never before had she wanted so badly to find the answers to those kinds of questions—with any man. She wondered if he could see it in her. Could he read her mind when he looked in her eyes?

Can you see how badly I want you to kiss me again?

Because she was rapidly becoming obsessed by it.

If he kissed her again he was in big trouble. Any number of the varying versions of silent oaths he'd made not to take advantage of their proximity would go right out the window. And little may she know, but the way she was looking at him was encouraging him to do just that. Forget every last one of them.

Every passing day with her it was becoming more and more of a physical need, but she was too amazing to be treated like a holiday fling. And it wasn't as if there could be any kind of a future in it. Not as if she'd be taking on the man she thought she was. In a scant few years he'd be someone drastically different from the man he was now. What right had he to take something that big from her when, from what he could tell, she'd already given up so much?

Ronan was many things, stupid wasn't one of them. All it had taken after his bout of uncharacteristic eavesdropping was a few carefully placed questions dropped in at seemingly random places in their daily conversations and he'd painted what he considered to be a fairly accurate picture of the kind of person Kerry Doyle was. And what it came down to was she was a giver.

Simple things would have indicated it. If someone was struggling with a door, she held it open for them with a smile. If someone looked as if they needed a seat more than she did, she gave it up with a smile. If a kid dropped something she would run after them for miles to kneel down and place it back in their little hands—*with a smile*.

She was constantly observant and on alert for those things and yet never complained when someone was rude or jumped a place in a line or let a door swing shut before she got to it. Though the smile wouldn't be quite so bright, he'd noticed…

Yes, Ronan had noticed all those things even before he'd started learning anything about her family and they'd made him like her even more than he already had.

And that was before he took into consideration the openness he'd liked from the beginning—not just in the way she would let excitement or pleasure or joy light up her face when they went somewhere new. Oh, no, she wasn't afraid to show deeper emotions either. Like in the Italian place he'd taken them to for lunch—when she'd listened to the owner sing opera and been so touched her eyes had filled with tears.

It had yanked him straight out of the morbidity he'd felt

himself sliding into only seconds before he'd looked at her. And he might have teased her about it, but he'd been completely charmed by the fact she was so emotive. Everything was on the surface with Kerry. Too many women played games in his experience; hiding who they really were in an attempt to make whatever they considered the 'right impression' on the man they were spending time with. But not Kerry.

Kerry was who Kerry was and she wasn't pretending to be anything else. Well, barring the fact she came from the wealthy background she did. Not that he could throw stones in that department.

And when he'd figured out who she was, he'd been stunned by the irony. She had no way of knowing how many times their paths must have crossed at home. He'd even bet his father had known her father at some point. Probably still did. It was a small country, after all.

Yet Ronan had never met Kerry. Mind you, he could probably put that down to the number of times he'd been home in the last decade. And when he had he'd had a scant couple of months to play 'catch up' so he could clear the decks to get away again—to pack as much travelling in while he was still able—so there hadn't been a whole heap of time for meeting new people.

He'd have remembered meeting Kerry.

With his gaze still tangled with hers, he couldn't help but feel exactly the way he had when he'd met her on the plane during the second leg of the flight to New York: wishing there were more time.

How many amazing places could he have shown her? How many things could he have seen with the same sense of magic he had the very first time simply because he was seeing them through *her eyes*? How many nights would there have been for long, languid sessions of—?

Well, suffice to say if he were the kind of man to let himself wallow in bitterness he'd have been doing it for not having those chances with someone like her.

But the specialist in New York had put paid to any glimmer of hope he had left so this trip with her was his last chance to escape facing up to reality.

Cowardly? *Probably.*

He could hear the husky edge in his voice when he spoke, echoing his intense desire to accept the silent invitation she was unconsciously issuing to be kissed.

'I'll make it up to you.' He silently cleared his throat and spoke in a steadier, intimately low tone. 'You tell me what fantasies didn't make it off that list of yours this time round and I'll see what I can do about fulfilling them. How does that sound?'

Kerry looked him straight in the eye—and the smouldering heat he saw in hers hit him so hard it was like being kicked in the chest.

Heaven help him—had she added being with him to her list? Because if she had—he wasn't so sure he had the strength to deny her. Not when he wanted her as badly as he did while she looked at him like that.

'You're gonna try and fulfil all my fantasies inside three months, are you?'

Even her voice did him in. He'd bet in decades to come that if he heard a voice remotely like hers, even in darkness, he'd feel drawn towards the sound.

Why did he have to meet someone like her now? What kind of sick cosmic joke was that? Ronan dearly wanted to hit something—*hard.*

Her head tilted to one side, finely arched brows then lifted a minuscule amount as she searched his eyes, as if she could see inside him and knew something was wrong.

He sincerely hoped she couldn't. And just to be sure, he smiled a slow smile at her, his fingertip tracing the answer to her question on her palm.

'Y—E—S—'

Kerry's moist lips parted in surprise, her gaze dropping to her hand as he finished tracing the 'S' and then rising as he smiled a larger smile at her.

She laughed huskily—the sound doing all kinds of amazing things to his libido.

Amazing. He thought it about her more and more with each passing day. And he wanted to be the man to fulfil at least some of those fantasies. Who could blame him?

'Tell me *all* of them.'

'My fantasies?' She waited long enough for him to nod— just the once. 'And then where would my sense of feminine mystique be, hmm?'

She quirked her brows, this time in challenge, a teasing light diluting some of the heat that'd been so palpable in the air between them. 'I gotta have something to work with to keep me interesting for the next couple of months, don't I?'

'You're interesting enough already.'

'You might not think so if you knew me better.'

He shook his head, reluctantly freeing her hand and leaning back in his seat as he mumbled his reply beneath his breath. 'I doubt it.'

Lifting his napkin from his knees, he nodded at her cup. 'Do you want to finish that? We have a way to go tomorrow and an early start, so—'

'Yes, an early night sounds good.' When her words translated into an innuendo regarding the activities people could get up to on 'early nights', his gaze locked with hers again, and he was rewarded with a dimpled, mischievous smile in return. 'I'm done.'

Good, because so was he—fighting the constant daily battle against his attraction to her was hard work. The sooner she was tucked safely away in her room, the better.

He made it all the way to the doors of their rooms, only

briefly checking up and down the wide hallway before he made the mistake of looking in her eyes again.

Bad move.

Because when her long lashes rose and she looked at him with the same silent invitation she'd issued over the table he could feel himself weakening, the memory of the one kiss they'd shared slamming into the front of his brain, his gaze dropping to her lips just as she damped them with the tip of her tongue.

Give him strength. Wanting her was *selfish*.

Her voice was breathless. 'If you aren't going to kiss me, then you have to leave—right now—before I do something I'll be embarrassed about in the morning.'

He looked back into her eyes. 'Not a modern-thinking, take-the-initiative-yourself kinda gal, then, I take it?'

'That's why you'd have to leave.'

'Before *you* kiss *me*?'

Her throat convulsed, her perfect teeth chewing on her lower lip as she nodded. 'If you want us to just stay friends on this trip, then I'm okay with that, but I need to know so I don't—'

'It's not that I don't want to—'

She stepped forwards and Ronan frowned hard, lifting his hands to her bare arms to physically set her away from him, his voice gruff. 'But it's probably better we don't. We have half a planet to get round yet and this would complicate things.'

The brief flash of agony in her eyes before she lowered her lashes almost did him in. She must be mortified. She'd just made it plain she wanted him to kiss her and he'd turned her down.

Her throat convulsed and she took a deep breath that lifted her breasts before her lashes rose. Then she smiled a smile that didn't quite make it all the way up into her eyes. 'You're right.'

Unfurling his fingers so he was brushing them over the soft

skin of her arms was hardly helping him make his case. 'I'm not the man for you, Kerry, Kerry Doyle. Trust me.'

Smaller hands appeared, wrapping around his fingers and lowering his hands all the way back down to his sides before letting go. 'Travel light—I know. Goodnight, Ronan.'

Stepping back, he watched as she turned to slide her card into the slot on her door, his eyes studying the smooth curtain of her hair while he fought to breathe evenly. He should turn away, he should go into his own room and forget this had happened, he should remind himself of all the reasons why he couldn't let her get involved with him, he should—

He stood still and watched her walk through the door. He watched it close in his face. And for a long while he just stood there listening to the thud of his heart as it beat hard against the wall of his chest until he finally found the strength to walk away.

But it cost him.

CHAPTER SIX

AFTER two more overheard conversations Ronan thought her family sounded as if they were a right pain in the—well, suffice to say if they kept interrupting the great effort he'd been making to keep Kerry smiling the way he'd finally managed to after the 'almost kiss' in San Francisco, then her phone was in great danger of being tossed in the next available body of water…

He glanced down at the top of her head, smiling at the fact she'd fallen asleep on his shoulder. It was a first for him on any kind of a plane—but then, somewhat miraculously, he was experiencing a lot of firsts with her around.

She made a small sigh in her sleep, nestling closer, and Ronan allowed himself to tuck her head beneath his chin even though she wouldn't get to doze for long, his gaze fixing on the few wisps of curling white clouds peppering the clear blue sky and the glimpses of azure blue sea beyond the tempered glass.

The irony was, if he'd managed to put all the pieces together correctly, they hadn't had that different an upbringing. Not really. Even with the common Irish bond removed…

The differences would only really appear at the point where she'd given up a lot of her own dreams to take on a role she might never have wanted if it hadn't been for the dramatic loss of half her family in one fell swoop. Whereas Ronan had arranged straight off that he'd always have the freedom to do the things he wanted to do—regardless of the responsibilities he held as heir apparent or the restrictions he would have to learn to live with in due enough course. Restrictions he was reminded of even as he looked out the window, the clear blue surrounded by a circle of black nothingness.

Kerry was living his life in reverse.

It was another reminder of why he shouldn't allow himself to get involved with her. Only trouble was he had a sneaking suspicion it was too late for him not to. The damage was already done, and was getting worse by the day. In fact, if he was honest with himself, he was now well into the region of *damage control*. She was already under his skin.

Kerry moved beneath his chin again, so he ducked back to try and see if she was waking up. And he was glad he'd decided to make the next leg of their journey a complete break for both of them—she needed the rest after their hectic country-hopping schedule so far, and it gave Ronan a chance to tick another person off his list while they were on this side of the globe.

Then there was the added bonus of yet another week full of golden opportunities to see Kerry in the bikini she'd worn in Hawaii. As far as Ronan was concerned she could live in it and he'd be more than okay with that. She was sensational. Luxury sports cars all over the planet could be sold in their millions if she lay across the bonnet in that bikini…

Even if seeing her in it tested his resolve to its absolute breaking-point. The first day she'd appeared in it he'd even groaned aloud—thankfully far enough away from her that she hadn't heard it. And he'd had to head straight for the water to hide the visible evidence of what the sight had done to him.

The pilot glanced down at the island beneath their wings,

jerking his thumb twice to say they were arriving, so Ronan gently nudged Kerry.

'Wake up, sleepyhead, or you'll miss it.'

He watched mesmerized as she came to life—her eyelids heavy the way they'd been after he'd kissed her that one time and the varying shades of russet and gold still endearingly soft with the sleep he could hear in her voice.

'Already?'

'Already.' He lifted his hand, curling his fingers under her chin to direct her gaze to the windows. 'Look.'

Kerry leaned forwards as she forced her eyes to focus. And when they did her breath caught at the beauty of it. Through the struts of the four-seat aircraft she saw something she'd doubted she'd ever see: a genuine South Sea island complete with fringe of white coral sand and a blue lagoon. It was the most beautiful thing she'd ever seen—a fantasy come true—and her voice was husky with more than sleep when she spoke, her hand unconsciously reaching for Ronan's to squeeze his fingers.

'Oh, you did *good* with this one. It's amazing!'

'I take it you like, it then?'

'No—I *love* it!'

'Can tick off another fantasy, can I?'

She laughed. 'You most definitely can.'

Tucked neatly into what Ronan had told her was the Yasawa chain of islands, the small resort had seemed like an impossible dream of a place when he'd finally got round to telling her about where they were going next. But the truth was he could have told her they were headed to the worst place in the universe and she probably wouldn't have complained. She'd already had such a good time destination-wise she almost had to pinch herself just to make sure she wasn't dreaming, even if it had taken several days for her to get over the toe-curling embarrassment of his rejection in the hallway.

But this trip was the first chance for her to grab hold of life with both hands and enjoy what the world had to offer and she couldn't let the fact she felt like a teenage girl with a crush around him get in the way.

She looked over her shoulder and felt her breath catch in her lungs at the sight of his face so close to hers. Then she glanced down and realized she still had his hand. Oh, she just didn't know when to stop. Wasn't one rejection enough for her?

So she let go and flashed a smile before looking back out the window—because she needed the distraction and because it was pointless dwelling on how very attracted she still was to him. She couldn't make him want her.

They splashed down, turning in one gliding motion from aircraft to boat, and then the pilot cut the engine.

'You'll need to carry your shoes or they'll get ruined wading in.'

Kerry aimed a sideways look at him as he moved away from her, blinking innocently. 'Yes, and it's not like I have that many shoes to sacrifice these days, is it?'

'And look how much faster we get on and off planes as a result of that. You're welcome, by the way.'

'I didn't say thank you.'

He smiled lazily. 'Yeah, but I know you meant to—so you're welcome.'

He took the shoes from her as she left the small plane, and with the other hand held hers as they waded side by side towards a cluster of Fijians waving a large welcome banner. Kerry giggled like an excited schoolgirl as their feet sank into the perfect white sand and the reception committee crowded round, grinning and forcing Ronan to free her hand as they pressed green coconuts towards them—complete with straw, hibiscus flower and slice of orange.

'*Bula!* Welcome!'

It was off the fantasy Richter-scale as far as Kerry was concerned. There was no way Ronan could top this one. He couldn't possibly.

A tall, ridiculously tanned man stepped out of the crowd and greeted Ronan with a manly hug before holding him at arm's length and announcing in an Aussie accent, ''Bout time too! Been too long.'

'It has.' Ronan lifted his hands to the man's shoulders, genuine affection written all over his face as he shook him. 'Good to see you, Frank.'

The older man's expression looked anguished for a brief second before being covered by a broad smile. 'You too, mate. I'm glad you can see the place one more time—me and Abbie been saying it would mean the world to us if you got to before—'

'This is Kerry,' Ronan interrupted him, dropping his hands to step back and draw Kerry forwards. 'I told you about her on the phone.'

Frank swiftly hauled her forwards to enfold her in a tight hug that stole her breath away, rocking her from side to side before he let go and placed her at arm's length to examine her face. 'Well, now—aren't you a pretty one?'

He cocked an eyebrow at Ronan, 'Didn't mention *that* on the phone…'

'Bad line from Nadi…' He carefully removed Kerry from Frank's hands and drew her back towards him. 'And you're a happily married man, so behave. Now do you have a spare bure for us or are we sleeping on the beach?'

Kerry tensed when he slung an almost possessive arm across her shoulders. Not that she actually had a problem with the subtle act of territorialism, but it was somewhat baffling—what was he doing? And why was he doing it? He'd already stated his friend was a happily married man so it wasn't as if he had to worry any—not that he would have even if the man had been single and a bit of a charmer—but hadn't he already made it plain as day they weren't anything more than friends? She didn't get it.

Actually, in fairness, for a man who claimed he wasn't the man for her he had a bit of a problem with not flirting with her too—that hadn't stopped. But he hadn't felt the need to touch her let alone tuck her in against the length of his lean body, until now. Was he simply demonstrating that they were friends?

Kerry's head was starting to ache.

Maybe she wasn't the first woman he'd brought to the island and this was him living up to his reputation?

Kerry was happier with the first option. But she had a deep and burning need to know just what exactly *had* been said on the phone now…

Frank led them across the perfect shoreline towards a chalet tucked into trees on one side and overlooking impossibly clear water on the other, chattering away to Ronan about the changes they'd made to the resort since his last visit. Meanwhile Kerry, while still listening with one ear, couldn't help but be mesmerized by her surroundings at the same time—and to think, they had an entire week in this place!

'She always this quiet?'

Ronan chuckled deep in his chest. 'I wish.'

Kerry nudged him hard in the ribs before smiling at Frank. 'This place is amazing, Frank.'

He beamed. 'I'm glad you approve.' Then he winked at her. 'And you must be somethin' for this bloke to be hauling you all the way out here to meet us. We always had to endure him alone before this.'

Well, that answered one question, then.

'Thanks for that, my friend.' Ronan shook his head. 'Though if you recall I visit for Abbie's cooking and the great view—not for your sparkling repartee…'

Kerry had another wink aimed her way. 'I save that for the ladies; it's wasted on him.'

She laughed.

So Ronan used the arm around her shoulders to pull her closer and stage-whisper in her ear, 'You'll have to forgive him—he doesn't get out much.'

'And if Abbie thought I'd get to meet women like you on a plane then I'd never get to leave the island again.' He scowled at Ronan, 'You're a lucky dog.'

Astonishingly Ronan didn't correct him.

Inside the bure Kerry stepped out of his hold to look around, turning in slow circles and moving in and out of open doorways as she took in everything from the high vaulted thatched-roof ceiling, separate sitting room and sunken Jacuzzi to the verandah with its day bed and private fish pond. Eventually stopping to stare at the hand-carved four-poster bed— her mouth suddenly dry as a world of possibilities opened up to her furtive imagination.

One bedroom.

'I'll take the day bed—you can have the fantasy bed and I'll tick that one off my list too.'

'Don't forget to leave a small light on at night,' Frank added without so much as a reaction to Ronan's clear announcement they weren't 'together', 'or you might fall in the Jacuzzi. *Again.* Not that it had anything to do with the lack of a light last time…'

Kerry lifted her brows in question as she looked at Ronan. 'You *didn't*—one cocktail too many, perchance?'

He didn't look the least little bit embarrassed about it either, jerking his head in the direction of the doorway. *'His fault.'*

Wandering casually in his direction, Kerry leaned her head towards his shoulder to inform him, 'Your halo's crooked.'

A loud burst of male laughter greeted her as she got to the doorway. 'Oh, *I like her.* Bring her back any time.'

When Ronan shot her a look that said she was in trouble, Frank took the opportunity to depart. 'Wander over when you're settled in—cocktail hour at the usual time—nice to meet you, Kerry.'

'You too, Frank.' She smiled as he left, aware of the very second Ronan stood beside her, her pulse dancing a salsa in reaction the way it always did.

There was a very brief moment of silence. And then a low, gruffly rumbled, 'Crooked, huh?'

Kerry laughed, the laughter turning to a shriek of surprise when Ronan suddenly wrapped his arms round her waist and lifted her off her feet. 'Put me down, you idiot—where are we going? You better not—*Ronan*—don't you *dare!*'

He bent over and unceremoniously dumped her into the Jacuzzi, water sloshing up over the edges and into her face so she was blinking furiously and still laughing loudly when the water splashed again as he joined her.

Kerry laughed all the more, if somewhat nervously, now he had them both in a Jacuzzi—fully clothed—as if it were something people everywhere did every day of the week. And her pulse rate went off the chart with him so close, her mouth suddenly dry.

He splashed water in her face. 'Welcome to paradise.'

Kerry blinked the water away, impulsively lifting her hands to ruffle his wet hair until it settled into dozens of opposing damp spikes. 'You're clinically insane—you know that, don't you?'

He studied her eyes for the longest while with arms outstretched, his fingers playing on the surface of the water. And it was torture, really it was. Didn't he have any idea what he did to her? Couldn't he hear how loudly her heart was beating? It certainly sounded loud to her.

'What do you want to do first?'

Now *there* was a question.

She swallowed hard. 'What are my options?'

His gaze dropped to her mouth and Kerry had to stifle a groan. *He was killing her!* And when he looked back up into her eyes she could see how the deeper blue had darkened in amongst the varying shades of his—realization hitting her like a blow to the chest.

He'd just thought about kissing her, hadn't he?

In the hall he'd said it wasn't that he didn't want to, but he'd been so *determined*—

She couldn't do it again. Once had been humiliating enough. So she wasn't going to open her mouth and take another chance, but that didn't mean she couldn't push him a little—just to see what happened. Maybe not the best plan in the greater scheme of things—but the brand-new, adventurous version of Kerry wanted to know…

She let herself float towards him. 'I guess I could dig my bikini out and go lie on the beach…'

Ronan floated back from her. 'We could go snorkelling—the sea-life here is pretty spectacular.'

'We could.' She had a sudden mental image of his lean, muscular body in his wet suit when he tried, unsuccessfully it should be said, to teach her to surf in Hawaii…Dear lord, but it had been hard not to gape at him…

He nodded firmly. 'Frank can teach you to dive if you like.'

She smiled impishly 'Are you looking to get rid of me?'

He made a sudden move, hauling himself up onto the edge of the tub. 'I'm going to go find where our stuff is.'

Kerry felt a bubble of joy rise inside her when he swiftly bounced to his feet. Oh, he wasn't as immune to her as he was letting on, was he? And even though she knew he'd been right about not wanting to complicate things she chose to ignore the fact that getting any further involved with him was pointless as she scrambled ungracefully out of the water to follow him.

"You know by now that I trust you, right?"

'I promise not to let you drown snorkelling.'

'Do you trust *me*?'

'Why, are you the first Irish female serial killer?'

'No—'

'Married?'

'*No.*' She scowled at his back. 'Would I be traipsing around the world with you if I was?'

'I'd certainly hope not.' A few feet away from her he turned, water dripping off his clothes and onto the wooden floor as he frowned at her. 'Where exactly are we going with this?'

Kerry took a deep breath, planting her hands on her hips. 'I'm curious.'

'About what?'

'About why it is you think I couldn't handle a holiday fling with you.'

He growled beneath his breath. 'Kerry—'

'No, come on—explain it to me. You said in San Francisco it wasn't that you didn't want to kiss me—'

'I explained why it wasn't a good idea,' And he said the words through clenched teeth so she knew she was touching a nerve. 'And it's still not.'

'You think I'd automatically expect a long-term commitment from you, don't you?' Her brows lifted with the question.

Ronan's hands bunched into fists at his sides. 'Woman—don't push me.'

She pushed. 'Are you gay?'

It was the most ridiculous question on the face of the earth—but she knew it would get a reaction. And did it ever, Ronan stepping towards her with anger rippling off every muscle,

'Did it *seem like I was* when I was kissing you in Times Square?'

Kerry shrugged her shoulders, her heart beating fast enough to have run a marathon. 'Are *you* married, then?'

A question that could really have done with being asked a lot sooner if she'd had a single doubt in her mind, which she hadn't—but it too had the desired effect, Ronan now looking as if he might genuinely strangle her.

His voice rose. 'Would I be traipsing around the world with *you* if I was?'

'I'd certainly hope not.'

He stopped in front of her, his jaw clenching, hands still in fists by his sides and Kerry almost baulked—almost. But she'd had weeks' worth of pent-up frustration building inside her and maybe she'd have coped with that eventually if he'd seemed completely uninterested—but he hadn't.

Not completely. While he was standing towering over her with heat radiating off his large body she thought about every single intense look, the number of times he'd looked at her mouth—both of which she'd put down to wishful thinking, particularly since his rejection. And she began to wonder if it *had* been wishful thinking.

She searched his eyes, her voice lowering. 'But you think I can't handle this, right?'

He stayed silent.

She kept her voice calm. 'You think this is easy to do after you rejected me last time? I'm risking humiliation on a scale hitherto unknown to womankind here. But I need to know—'

'Need to know *what?*'

Her chin rose. 'If I'm the only one fighting this!'

'You think I'm not fighting this every damn day?'

The words were thrown at her with such force that she knew they'd been dragged up from deep inside him. And it tore her up inside to know she wasn't the only one suffering, her vision blurring in response.

'Then why are we fighting?' When her voice wavered on the words she swallowed hard and took a deep breath before continuing, 'We're both adults, Ronan.'

Ronan lifted both hands and rubbed them down over his face, muffling a groan before he dropped them and looked her in the eye, his deep voice rough. 'Kerry, if I kiss you there's a very good chance I won't be able to stop. It's not you I don't trust—it's me.'

Her lips trembled, forming a smile. 'What makes you think I'd want you to stop, you idiot?'

'Kerry—' her name sounded like a plea, his large hands lifting to frame her face as he leaned forwards to look into her eyes more closely '—there's no happily ever after with me.'

Kerry lifted her hands and placed them on his, holding his intense gaze. 'Did I ask you for one?'

'You deserve one.'

Her heart filled her chest. 'I'd settle for happy in the here and now. Most people would these days.'

Ronan shook his head, and she could see the control he was exerting over himself—it was written all over him. 'You deserve *more*.'

'How about you let *me* decide?'

'Kerry—'

'You can use my name as many times as you like, but now I know you feel the same way—'

He silenced her the way she'd been aching for him to all along—the kiss anything but gentle—and Kerry practically fell into him, her knees giving way under the onslaught of so much released frustration. His lips were hard and bruising, but she didn't care, her hands moving to grip hold of his shoulders while she released her own frustration and responded with all the need she'd been holding inside.

When he rocked forwards, his hands dropped, arms wrapping around her and holding her tighter against the hard length of his body while he pillaged her mouth. And Lord alone knew how much further they'd have gone if one of the staff hadn't appeared with their bags—clearing his throat loudly from the doorway.

Ronan wrenched his mouth from hers, setting her firmly

away from him and turning to shelter her from prying eyes before he cleared his throat.

'Thanks.'

Kerry fought to control her breathing until he turned again, her heart still running a marathon and her pulse skittering through her veins while he looked down at her face. If he even thought about trying to reject her now she might have to kill him.

His hands rose to her face again, thumbs smoothing over her cheeks. 'Are you okay?'

She laughed softly. 'Little shaky on my feet, if I'm honest. But yes.'

'Good.' He smiled a deliciously slow smile. 'What am I going to do with you woman?'

Kerry bit her lip to stop laughing again and Ronan shook his head in reply.

'That's not what I meant.'

The laughter escaped.

And he shook his head again, thumbs still smoothing against her cheeks. 'I think we should go find some nice colourful fish to look at before we go rushing into anything, don't you?'

'Probably.'

The smile grew. 'Don't pout.'

He leaned in and brushed his mouth over hers, a mere whisper of a kiss when compared to the onslaught from moments before, his voice then rumbling against her swollen lips. 'Go get changed.'

Kerry followed him when he tried to lean back, brushing her mouth over his the same way he just had, her eyes wide open and staring into his. 'No more fighting, okay? What happens happens…'

'One step at a time.'

It was exactly what she'd meant. And she'd already pushed more than enough. She just had to pray she hadn't got herself in over her head…

* * *

'She doesn't know, does she?'

Ronan took a deep breath before dropping another carrot into the pan of salted water. 'No, and it's staying that way.'

'Ronan—'

The warning edge to Abbie's soft voice drew his gaze up to lock with hers before she could go any further. 'There's no point in her knowing.'

'You like her—a lot.'

He smiled ruefully. And Abbie nodded before turning her attention back to the artistic endeavors required for the kind of dessert Ronan would merrily sell a limb for. Abbie's famous desserts had been one of the things that firmly placed the island into Ronan's idea of heaven on earth from his first visit. It was why he never flew over their side of the planet without dropping in, even if it was only for twenty-four hours and an extra helping of dessert he could take with him to Nadi—to eat in the airport while he waited for another flight to wherever he was going.

Well, that on top of the fact they were some of the first friends he'd made when he took up travelling. And had remained two of the best ever since.

'She like *you* as much?'

'Now, Abbie…'

'Oh, don't bother pulling out that patented charm of yours for me, young man. I'm the one woman on the planet it doesn't work on and you know it.'

'Well, if you're the only one then that kinda answers your question for you, doesn't it?'

She threw a scowl at him, the twitch of her lips and the glow of affection in her eyes diluting it enough for him to know he wasn't in any real trouble, so he went back to the mountain of carrots she'd handed him.

But Abbie wasn't done, her voice filled with false nonchalance. 'Interesting that she's the first woman you've brought here, don't you think?'

'I thought she'd enjoy it.'

'Everyone enjoys it here—that's not why you brought her. You brought her 'cos this place has a special place in your heart and you wanted to share that with her. You *like* her.'

'You already told me I do—' he wasn't playing and she should know better '—so it must be true.'

The end of a wooden spoon was waved above the carrots, immediately catching his attention and lifting his gaze to follow the chocolate-coated implement as it was waved back and forth in warning.

'You don't fool me for a single second so you can just stop that. If you like her then why don't you take a chance and let her in?'

'You done with that spoon?'

It was held up so the chocolate began a temptingly slow downward path. 'You can have the spoon when you answer the question.'

'Fine, then.' He frowned as he let the words slip free on a flat tone he knew rightly wouldn't fool her. 'I don't need a nursemaid just yet, that's why.'

When he reached for the spoon she lifted it higher, a look of disbelief on her face. 'You think she'd stay with you because she felt sorry for you? What kind of woman did you bring to my island?'

'That chocolate is gonna drip all over the place in a minute—seems like an awful waste to me.'

'Ronan!'

With a deeply heartfelt sigh, he dragged his gaze from the chocolate to a random point at his left, digging deep to keep his patience and not howl at the sky the way he felt like doing. 'It's my choice not to tell her, Abs. I don't have to explain why. Leave her out of it—she's—well, she's—'

'I got that after ten minutes with her.'

He nodded. He'd always considered his friends fairly good judges of character. They were *his* friends after all, he always told them—that showed how good at judging they were…

'How are you managing to hide it?'

Actually it had taken some pretty intensive forward planning, which could only be a good thing in the long run, he felt—a practice run of sorts. He'd learned how to use his vast knowledge of their destinations to avoid dimly lit places at night, how to make sure he always gave her plenty to look at so she wouldn't focus too much on him—and so far so good. All he had to do was maintain the deception all the way back to the Emerald Isle and he'd be grand. She'd never have to know and he'd never have to see pity in her eyes.

He opened his mouth to voice the one concern he'd had about bringing her here. 'I might need you and Frank to help me some later. You still eat in the dark by hurricane lamp, right?'

He knew she knew what he was aiming at when her hand reached across and squeezed his, her voice threaded thick with emotion. 'Already?'

'Just don't go letting me make a fool of myself.'

'We won't.' She handed him the spoon.

'See—now that's why I love you, though in fairness you get extra points over Frank for the desserts.'

'You're incorrigible.'

'Yeah, someone else tells me that these days too.'

CHAPTER SEVEN

KERRY felt her idea of heaven on earth now came down to a few basics.

Having every whim indulged, whether it be a horseback ride along white sands just before sunset or being taken to a desert island by boat where they could wade ashore and spend a full day completely alone; picnicking on the selection of lobster, buttered rolls, salad, pineapple, pawpaw and a jug of watermelon juice beaded with moisture Abbie packed for them—even though Ronan complained bitterly about the lack of desserts.

And then there were the hours whiled away floating across acres of yellow coral waving with the surge of the sea, with shoals of black and white damselfish looking very much like mint humbugs to Kerry as they swam by, and bright red and white clownfish poking their faces out of sea anemones while a yellow and black angelfish picked a fight with a blue-striped wrasse. Ronan informed her of all their names when they would surface for air and she would describe them amidst bursts of bubbling laughter when he laughed at how breathless she was from trying to stay under as long as possible without drowning.

Then there was the hammock specifically tailored for two Ronan decided they should adopt for after Abbie's delicious lunches. They would lie gently swaying together, the sea breeze wafting over them as they shared the most embarrassing stories from their childhoods or the worst dates they'd ever been on or he'd wheedle more off her fantasy destinations list and tell her about them if he'd been there—the majority of which he of course had—and sometimes they'd even get round to discussing things he could put in the book they both seemed to have so conveniently forgotten since they'd got there. All of it interspersed by soft, exploratory kisses that went on for ever...

Heaven on earth.

But even with all those wonderful experiences and memories it was only truly heaven on earth for Kerry because Ronan was there—it was sharing everything with him that made the experiences into *moments* she would remember for the rest of her life.

She was falling hard for him.

It was the atmosphere, she told herself. It was the romance of the island, she reasoned. It was sharing so many magical experiences she could only have dreamed of—she'd tried using every one of them as an explanation for the way her heart would positively glow with warmth every time she looked at him.

But it was him.

And she couldn't seem to stop it from creeping up on her, which only served to make the aching inside her grow—especially in the darkness of their bure at night, when she would listen for any sound of him moving on the day bed while she lay alone in the huge four-poster bed meant for two.

They had two full days and three nights left in heaven. And she really didn't want the something to keep them apart any more—even if she had to let him go in the end.

'If you care about him as much as I think you do don't give up on him just yet. Be patient.' Abbie's words still whispered in the back of her mind, long after the walk back from dinner...

The dinner get-together had rapidly become another favourite memory for Kerry to keep. With Frank presiding over the long table set out under a banyan tree, lit by hurricane lamps and decorated with pots of orchids, she'd felt welcomed into their tight-knit group from the very first night as they filled the balmy night air with laughter and the warmth of the open love Ronan obviously shared with his friends. And Ronan hadn't been the least bit behind the door about touching her in front of them, tangling her fingers with his, wrapping an arm around her waist to draw her closer after he'd abandoned all pretence at conversation with the arrival of Abbie's chocolate truffle cake, which to Kerry's secret inner chocoholic's glee turned out to be a milk chocolate pudding and white chocolate ice cream drizzled with dark chocolate sauce—*bliss!*

Though she'd soon learned the arm-around-her-waist trick was a way for Ronan to sneak some of her portion as well as his own by tickling her ribs.

But he'd been more than happy for his friends to accept her as being 'his'. And she'd felt her confidence grow because of it.

By the third night he'd taken to leaning in close to say something in a deliciously intimate rumbling voice that tickled the sensitive skin on her neck. Or he'd tuck her hair behind her ear. Or press his lips to her temple—sometimes simply aiming the kind of intense heated look at her that had her glancing around the table to see if anyone else had noticed what he'd done to every single one of her nerve endings…

By the fourth night it was Abbie she found watching them nearly every single time she checked. Sometimes with a look of open curiosity, sometimes with a small frown, sometimes with an affectionate smile that gave Kerry the hope she approved of what she saw.

A hope she had confirmed on their nightly stroll across the starlit beach to Ronan and Kerry's shared bure. With Ronan and Frank several feet ahead of them Abbie had linked their arms and smiled at the backs of the two men while she spoke.

'I'm glad he brought you to visit.'

'Me too—I can't tell you how much I've loved it. You're incredibly lucky living here together.'

'We think so too.' She squeezed Kerry's arm, 'You'll have to come back and see us again.'

'I will.' And she meant it, even if the very thought of visiting without Ronan was so painful it almost doubled her over. She really was going to have to get a better handle on her emotions.

'You're good together.'

Heat rose on her cheeks. 'Well, we're not actually—'

She didn't want Abbie to think there was more to it than there actually was. Or worse still for Abbie to say to *Ronan* that she thought there was. Because that wasn't the 'agreement', was it?

'Yes, you are—whether you choose to admit it or not.' She studied Kerry's face for a few steps, looking forward to check how close they were to the men before lowering her voice to add, 'If you care about him as much as I think you do don't give up on him just yet. Be patient.'

A light came on inside the bure.

Abbie turned to hug her as Frank reappeared, whispering above her ear, 'He can be hard work, I know—but he's worth it.'

Swallowing down a lump of emotion, Kerry managed a nod and a choked, 'I know he is.'

And she meant it. Even if she didn't see how a rolling stone like him could ever be happy with someone who could only wangle one trip a year at best.

Then Frank was there, kissing her on the cheek and wishing her goodnight before swinging his wife into his arms and waltzing her up the beach—the sound of their laughter echoing in the distance long after Kerry went into the chalet.

But she could still hear Abbie's voice in her head hours later when she heard Ronan moving on the day bed and she held her breath, straining to hear his breathing above the sound of the surf outside. Four nights she'd tried and she'd yet to hear it, but it didn't stop her trying.

'You're still awake, aren't you?'

He said it just softly enough that if she hadn't been he wouldn't have woken her. 'How did you know?'

'You weren't snoring.'

'I do *not* snore.' She turned onto her side and hauled the light cover up to her chin in indignation. 'And even if I did you shouldn't tell me I do.'

'There's another rule, is there?'

Her mouth curled into a smile. 'Yes, there is. And if there isn't there should be. Ladies aren't supposed to snore.'

'Betcha Nana snores like a trooper and doesn't care who knows it.'

The subject of Kerry's beloved nana had proved one of his greatest sources of amusement when they shared stories on the hammock…

'Nana is of an age where she says she's earned the right to do whatever she wants, no matter what people think or say. Or what they tell her she can't possibly do any more…'

There was only the briefest heartbeat of a pause before he answered, 'I think I'm a little in love with Nana. Think I'd stand a chance with her?'

She'd probably love him too. Didn't everyone?

'So why are you awake?'

'Why are you?'

'I asked first.'

'Can't sleep.'

Kerry rolled her eyes in the darkness, 'Well, duh.'

She was immediately rewarded with a deep chuckle of laughter. 'Now that's mature.'

'I've obviously been spending too much time with you.'

'I'd have come up with something more mature than that. I'll have you know I have an extensive vocabulary—and not just in the one language. I speak three types of *foreign* fluently.'

'Go on, then. Say something in *foreign* to me.'

'Okay.' She heard him moving around again, his voice a little closer when he eventually spoke—as if he'd turned so his head was now at the bottom end of the bed. '*Je n'ai avant jamais rencontré quelqu'un comme vous. Mais je suis très heureux que je vous ai rencontré.*'

How could his voice possibly manage to sound even sexier in French? It really wasn't fair.

'And what does that mean?'

'It means I promise not to tell you if you snore in the future…'

'That's good of you. *Je suis heureux je vous ai rencontré aussi. Même si vous dites le le mensonge impair d'éviter de dire réellement quelque chose de gentil à moi.*'

'Damn.' The smile came through in his voice. 'How's your Italian?'

'Well, you could tell me in Italian that you've never met anyone like me and you're glad you did—if you like. But I'll still answer that I'm glad I met you too—though maybe not as smoothly as in French.' She smiled into the darkness, her heart still swelling in her chest from his confession. 'We hoteliers tend to pick up the basics of popular modern-day "foreign".'

'And I s'pose you'll still tag on the fact you feel that way even when I lie to avoid admitting I said something nice?'

'You could be nice more often.'

'If you're not careful I'll come over there and show you just how nice *I can be*.'

'Promises, promises…'

The words were out before she could stop them. And when the bure went quiet she fought the instinctive need to curl into a partial foetal position to try and hold the groan of embarrassment inside. She couldn't believe she'd just said it—not that she hadn't meant it, but—

But what did he expect after all the kissing and touching and playing about in the sand and the hammock he loved so much? And that was before she took into account what he was doing to her poor heart on an almost daily basis. No wonder she—ached—the way she did most nights when she lay alone in a huge bed designed for honeymooners.

'If I come over there all the effort I've put into being as close to a gentleman as I get will leave this bure at great speed. I've seen that nightdress you're only just wearing.'

Kerry had to take a moment to swallow, lick her dry lips and control her breathing before she responded to the husky edge in his voice. 'You put this nightdress on the keeper pile—remember?'

He made a noise that sounded distinctly like a growl of warning. 'Catching glimpses of you wearing it is something altogether different—trust me.'

'You see me in a bikini every day.'

'I know. And that's exactly why I've had to put so much effort into being gentlemanly.'

'Not that you find me repulsive, then.'

'No.' He sighed impatiently into the darkness. 'If you were repulsive I wouldn't be having problems getting to sleep over here knowing you're over there wearing what you're wearing.'

The new-version Kerry couldn't help but push a little. 'I could take it off if that'd help.'

There was a distinct sound of movement swiftly followed by a muffled groan, which made Kerry smile ridiculously on her side of the room, her heart taking on an erratic rhythm at the thought of him struggling to stay where he was.

'Are you hiding under your pillow?'

'Woman!' His raised voice told her he'd come out of hiding, the frustrated edge telling her she was pushing him a step too far. 'I'm still trying not to make this thing between us any more complicated than it already is. *Help me out here.*'

'You're right.'

'I know I am.'

'It's already complicated.'

'Yes, it is.'

'And we have very different lives.'

'We do.'

'Once this trip is over there's absolutely no reason why our paths would cross. They didn't before.'

'*Exactly.*'

'We might never see each other again.'

'I know.' His voice dropped.

And she might have seen sense at that point if it hadn't held the edge of fatalistic resignation it had. But in the darkness she could feel it magnified tenfold—the *answering need* in him. She could feel it tugging at her soul from clean across the room.

Her voice shook on the words. 'Every fantasy on my list. That's what you wanted to give me, right?'

'Don't—' He sounded strangled.

'Thing is, somewhere along the way I think I've maybe added you to that list—' her breath hitched, her voice barely above a whisper as she tried to force the rest out while she still had the courage '—and every day we spend touching—and kissing— just, it just—well, it makes everything *more*—I guess…'

Oh, she was making a real mess of this, wasn't she?

'*Kerry*—'

'You see, I can't sleep over here on my own either, because—' She took a deep breath and tried again, the words tumbling out in a rush '—I guess I miss you beside me now

I've got so used to it. 'Cos when we're in the hammock in the afternoon I have no problem dozing off, do I? But in here I just spend all my time thinking about you all the way over there and I guess that means I must *need you* beside me and this aching—'

There was a loud thud followed by a muffled curse and a, 'Don't move. And don't *dare* take anything off—I *mean* it. I'm coming over there.'

Kerry held her breath, her heart thundering so loudly in her ears she could barely hear him until the bed dipped behind her and an arm snaked around her waist to bring her back against the hard length of his body where he lay above the covers. And for a long moment after he'd curled his knees into the backs of hers and rested his chin on the top of her head, she just lay there—waiting—until he took a deep, shuddering breath; as if it had cost him dearly to come to her when he'd been trying so hard not to.

It tipped her over the edge.

The aching in her chest finally broke free to form silent tears as with all her heart and soul she willed him to trust her—to believe in her and let her into his heart the way he'd wormed his way into hers…

'Don't cry.'

Kerry took a hiccupping breath, because she'd thought she'd done a pretty good job of not letting on she was.

He turned her in his arms so his breath whispered over her damp cheeks while he traced her face with impossibly tender fingertips. 'Don't cry—not because of me—you hear?'

The incredible softness in his husky voice reached out and wrapped around her aching heart. 'I hear.'

'And I can see you—even in the dark—did you know that?' His fingertips traced up to her hairline, over her temple, taking time with each arch of her brows while he continued in a low rumble that sneaked in around the edges of her soul. 'Right now I can see your face with the sun on it—the way you look when I see you every day; smiling the way you do. I can see all those things right this minute Kerry, Kerry Doyle. Just like I can lie in the dark every night and see you in this nightdress. Or half not in it, I should say. I can see *that* best of all…'

Her hiccupped breath was released on a soft burst of laughter. 'Still incorrigible.'

'Always.' His smile came through in his voice, his fingertips tracing each closed eye—lingering on the edges of her lashes for a while before tracing her nose, as if committing her face to memory by touch. 'So don't cry because of me.'

'I'm sorry.' She reached for him as she said it, turning her body into his, because she *was* sorry—sorry she'd ruined things a little by being so emotional in front of him. Everything had been so—right—since they'd come to the island. And now she'd taken a little of the magic away by not being able to leave things be.

'Don't do that either.' His fingertips had moved from her nose to her cheek, smoothing away any lingering moisture at the same time as he added the shape to whatever mental picture he was drawing. 'Don't ever apologize for being who you are. You feel things and you're never afraid to show you do. Most women don't do that second part, you know.'

Old-version Kerry hadn't either.

Even if she'd had the courage to tell him that, she wouldn't have been able to form the words, because by then his wandering fingertips had begun to trace her mouth—starting at the outer edges and following the shape until she parted her lips to draw in a breath. And then he traced the plumpness of her lower lip, taking a hint of moisture from inside the upper edge to dampen it before she felt the air displace above her face.

'Don't change. Just don't cry.'

The first kiss was so heartbreakingly gentle she sighed

against his mouth, breathing in when he breathed out—her hand settling palm-down on the heated skin of his bare chest, moving until she had it directly above the firm thudding beat of his heart below his breastbone.

She tilted her head back into the soft pillows to allow him better access—he then angled his head and hesitated for the briefest second before repeating the sliding touch of firm lips over soft. And they kissed like that for the longest time, the ocean beyond the walls of the bure the only sound beyond the joint breathing that changed by increments from deep and slow to shallower and quicker when soft kisses weren't enough any more—for either of them.

Ronan's large hand moved over the soft skin of her shoulders while the other toyed with the hair spread out on her pillow and Kerry's one hand remained constantly on the beat of his heart while she let the other trace each muscle in his arm from the wrist up—revelling in the sensuality of his distinct maleness and the delicious sense of femininity she felt magnified by the sheer size of his body laid out next to hers.

'Mmm,' he groaned against her now swollen lips.

'Mmm-hmm.' She smiled mid-kiss, unable to break the contact long enough to form coherent words.

Ronan groaned again, the sound deeper in his chest this time, vibrating beneath her palm. 'We…need to…'

'Mmm.'

'Kerry—'

Her hand had reached his wide shoulder, so she used it for leverage and rolled onto him, scrambling ungraciously through the light sheets as she stretched her body along the length of his, breasts squashed against his chest, her legs lined up with his—the only thing between them now a bundled lump of cotton and the sliding silk of her nightdress.

Ronan used both hands to frame her face, lifting her head back so he could break the kiss long enough to speak, his chest heaving beneath her. 'Kerry, we should stop. I promised myself I wouldn't let it go this far.'

She smiled into the darkness. 'Didn't want to take advantage of me, huh?'

He exhaled his answer. 'Exactly that.'

'Didn't talk to *me* about it tho', did you?'

'Not really a conversation starter.'

'Might possibly have come across a tad arrogant…'

His chest shook with silent laughter. 'Might.'

One large hand moved from her face to smooth down over her hair, past the bare skin of her shoulder to the smooth silk against the small of her back. And Kerry smiled all the more at the fact he couldn't stop touching her while he was trying to stop what they were doing. What was it they said about actions speaking louder?

It was gloriously empowering.

'Don't I get a say in it now?'

'Probably best not.'

She wriggled to get more comfortable and wanted to laugh aloud when he tensed underneath her—she could win this battle quite easily if she set her mind to it, couldn't she? And she'd never seduced a man before.

'Am I too heavy for you?'

'No.'

It sounded distinctly as if he was gritting his teeth. So she wriggled again, just to see…

Ronan growled. 'But you could *quit that*.'

'Wanna know what I think?' She rested her forearms on his bare chest.

'Not sure it's safe to find out—so, no.'

'What *I* think—' she stifled laughter when he made a deep sound of exasperation '—is that this partnership needs a little more equality.'

'Really.'

'Yes, you see so far I've tiptoed around you—'

That got her a burst of disbelieving laughter. 'Oh, have you indeed? God help me.'

She nudged both arms down a little. 'Yes—*I have*. But this is supposed to be *my* trip, isn't it?'

'It is.'

'Except that you've made the decision to call all the shots and have a go at fulfilling my fantasies along the way, haven't you?' She didn't give him a chance to interrupt. 'And I kinda love that, don't get me wrong—'

'But?'

'*But*—I don't need you to make every decision for me. I'm a big girl. What happens—happens, remember?' She took a huge breath of warm air and laid it on the line just in case he hadn't got it already. 'And I don't think you'd be over here if you weren't finding it equally tough as me to stop it from happening.'

'I think we've established that.'

'So why are we fighting it again, then?'

'Because I already care about you too much to hurt you— that's why.'

Kerry knew that. She'd probably have suspected it for a while if she were surer of herself, but the way he'd just been with her—with so much gentleness in his voice and his touch, and using words that would have broken through the most hardened of hearts…

She knew he cared.

'Know what Nana would say if she was here?'

'After she'd kicked me from here to next week for being in your bed, you mean?'

'Actually having met you she'd probably pretend she didn't know where you were while she imparted her words of wisdom. In fact—now I think about it—you said something similar to what she'd say on the plane that first time, about desserts.'

She could hear him shaking his head. 'Okay, crazy girl—I'll bite. What did I say?'

'Life's too short.'

He tensed underneath her again, the hand on her back stilling. So she lowered her voice and kept going, staying patient the way someone who knew Ronan better than she did had advised.

'And Nana would add that you should grab hold of happiness when you find it—no matter how short or long an amount of time it lasts.'

Ronan didn't speak, but tension rolled off him in waves and his heart was thundering beneath her arms. He was still fighting, wasn't he? She could feel it in him. And it was one hell of a battle. Kerry could sense that instinctively too. What she didn't get was why. She'd made it plain as the day was long that she wanted him—he obviously wanted her—and the kissing they'd been doing had been leading them to where they were for days.

'He can be hard work...but he's worth it.'

And he hadn't moved away. So Kerry took that as a positive sign and moved her arms to rest her head on his chest, her hands on his shoulders. Then she stayed there, simply because it was where she wanted to be—and because she wasn't giving up on him.

Ronan could take as long as he needed to think about what she'd said. She'd be patient. She'd wait. And she'd keep on letting him know she wanted him.

Because she felt he was worth it—and she loved him. She'd been falling since the first time she'd looked in those sensational eyes.

She was in well and truly over her head.

CHAPTER EIGHT

IT WAS time to leave the island. And, having spent forty-eight hours battling his needs, Ronan was uncharacteristically silent, and all too aware of the fact. As aware as he was of the fact Kerry had noticed too. Not that she'd pulled him on it. She seemed to know not to push him further than she already had and he was glad of it.

Fighting his own needs was one thing—fighting hers was something else entirely.

He also knew how much Frank and particularly Abbie were struggling to keep smiles on their faces. It was exactly the kind of thing he'd been trying to avoid since he'd decided to see as many of his friends as possible, the need to see them yet another reminder of his own selfishness? he wondered.

But it was *precisely* the kind of reminder he needed not to let Kerry any closer than she already was, even when every bone in his body desperately wanted him to. And reminders like that could never be thrown at him enough, because when it came to Kerry he was a weak man—a *very* weak man.

The Fijian staff draped garlands of hibiscus flowers around their necks and Frank and Abbie walked them all the way into the water. Ronan then watched with a constricting tightness in his chest as each of them hugged and kissed Kerry, Abbie whispering to her with tears glistening in her eyes—while

Ronan silently prayed she wasn't saying anything that might make it more difficult for him later on. Then, with Kerry safely in the seaplane, he waded back to say his own goodbyes, his mouth drawn into a narrow line when Abbie held him just a little too tight for just a little too long.

He managed a smile when he held her at arm's length, scowling at her with mock severity. 'Stop that. Just think of it this way—how you look now is how I'll always see you. You'll never age.'

When tears welled up in her eyes and splashed over her lashes he hugged her tight again, pressing a kiss to her temple as he forced his throat to work. 'Gorgeous for ever, Abs, even when I can't see your face any more.'

She sobbed, and Frank took her under one arm as Ronan turned away. He'd suffered through the worst of their goodbyes the night before and there really wasn't anything else to say.

One of the staff then made the last wading steps even tougher for him by strumming a guitar—all of them singing 'Ise Lei'—a sad farewell to Fiji.

Someone, somewhere really had it in for him.

On the plane, Kerry said nothing, she simply set her smaller hand in his, tangled their fingers and squeezed before the engine roared and they lifted off over the blue lagoon he knew he'd probably never see again.

'Open the window and throw your garland into the water— if it drifts ashore you'll return,' their pilot kindly threw back over his shoulder.

Making Ronan dearly want to beat him to death with a string of bright scented flowers…

Instead he let go of Kerry's hand to open the window while she lifted the garland over her head. Once it was dropped, she turned to him.

'Now you.' She waggled her fingers, making him think about the first time she'd asked to see his passport.

Not this time. He shook his head, lifting his to replace hers. 'Mine looks better on you. Let's just see if yours makes it back.'

Even if he did make it back, he wouldn't be the same man, would he? It wouldn't be the same experience.

The plane took its time rising, giving them just enough time to watch Kerry's garland float towards the beach, the sight bitter-sweet. But good, he told himself. He liked the idea of the people that mattered to him together on the island again some time in the future.

Now all he had to do was get through the next few weeks without Kerry cottoning onto why he was fighting. Somehow, knowing her as well as he did now, he doubted she'd see it the way he did. And there was no way she was changing his mind.

In the meantime he had plans for more fantasy fulfilment. Because if he was going to hurt her at the end of their three months together, then he was going to make sure every preceding second was a gateway to every adventure she ever took…

It was the best gift he could give her.

Kerry got suspicious when, off his own bat and without any persuasion, he suggested she went shopping in Sydney. 'What kind of things?'

He shrugged. 'A long dress, couple of smart casual outfits, pair of posh shoes if you really have to—which, knowing you, you will.'

'I *had* a long dress in San Francisco. But *someone* wouldn't let me keep it.'

He chose to ignore the fact he might actually have been wrong about something.

'You can stop somewhere and get your hair done too if you like. I have a few people to see while I'm here anyway so I'll be busy.' He set his hands on her shoulders, turned her round and then used the knuckles of one hand in the small of her back to nudge her towards the hotel-room door. 'Do you need money?'

'No—I have money—and I doubt your publisher's will swallow dresses and a hairdo as research expenses.'

'You'd be surprised what I can get away with.'

She stopped in the open doorway to frown at him. 'What's wrong with my hair?'

Ronan shook his head, smiling indulgently. 'There's nothing wrong with your hair. But you might want to swap the sexy beach look for something a tad more sophisticated for where we're going next. Or I'll pay the price for not warning you before we got there.'

'Where are we going?'

'It's a surprise.'

'I hate surprises.' It was a fib he'd most likely call her on but she *would* hate surprises if she wasn't at least marginally prepared for them—this was a new, and somewhat worrying development, especially if it involved her being pushed forcibly out the door to shop for clothes for a mystery destination. It was a woman's worst nightmare—didn't he know that? And it wasn't as if she could phone a friend to ask what everyone else would be wearing…

'You've loved every surprise I've come up with so far and you'll love this one too. Though frankly I can't believe it's taking this much effort to get you to go shopping.'

'It's been so long I'm worried I've forgotten how to do it.'

'I'm sure it'll come back to you.' He leaned in and kissed her, the woeful expression on her face apparently too much to resist. 'Now shoo. The sooner you go, the sooner you'll be back.'

She brightened. 'Meaning you'll miss me?'

'How can I miss you when you won't go away?'

He was entirely too clever for his own good. 'In that case I won't be back for ages. That way you can get an opportunity to miss me *bad*.'

His chin dropped and he sighed, making Kerry smile at the top of his head. Still fighting it—yes, showing signs of weakening though—she hoped. She just had to keep going and pray he got half as attached to her as she was to him. And if by some miracle he did, then they could maybe talk about the possibility of seeing each other any time he was home from one of his trips or—better still—about taking another trip together. She didn't want to clip his wings, but it didn't mean she didn't want more time.

Time more than anything. Because it was running out. They had ten days to 'do' some of Australia, three days in Hong Kong, a couple of days in Dubai on the way back and then Paris, because she'd promised Nana she'd be there on a certain date and it was the only thing she'd insisted Ronan couldn't change.

He'd told her on the flight from Fiji that he'd left any other short stops in Europe off his mental list because it was easy for her to get to on her own some time in the future. And it had hurt hearing it—especially when he'd said it so calmly; as if it didn't matter she'd be doing it without him.

'Be back before four or we'll be late.'

'Bully.'

'I'll revoke the shopping privileges if you're not careful. And you'll regret it when we get to the surprise…' He shot her a look that said 'on your own head be it, young lady'.

So Kerry silently admitted defeat before she lifted a hand—her thumb and forefinger creating a small space for her to squint through. '*Little clue* to help with my shopping decisions…?'

'Nope.' But an answering pout earned her another kiss. 'I'm helping you learn to roll with the punches and be spur-of-the-moment. You'll thank me later.'

The new Kerry could learn to be spur-of-the-moment; she felt she'd done very well with it so far…

But she got suspicious again when they reached his secret destination that evening—complete with all the purchases she was eternally grateful for when she walked onto the platform. What he'd allowed her in San Francisco during the 'travel light' lesson would never in a million years have seen her through a trip on Australia's version of the Orient Express. And she'd never have forgiven him for that.

She'd thought he'd have trouble topping the island experience but the Great South Pacific Express was close—completely different, but close when it came to the fantasy fulfilment he was so hell-bent on. The carriage interiors were rich and polished, a dazzling mixture of craftsmanship and comfort and old-fashioned—*opulence*—quite frankly. Which was why, when she discovered he'd booked them, not one, but *two* top-end cabins, she wasn't just suspicious about the fact he'd separated them at night again but about how exactly the huge expense was being dealt with. Something wasn't right, and she just couldn't quite put her finger on what it was…

After he'd made polite conversation about the area and the train all the way through a sensational dinner in one of the restaurant cars, Kerry mentally gritting her teeth to stop herself from starting an argument in front of such an elegant audience, they'd moved on to a lounge complete with baby grand piano. Then she calmly waited while tapping her toe on the carpeted floor, until they both had sparkling crystal glasses of a crisp Pinot in hand, before launching into the line of questioning she'd formulated.

'Tell me about this publisher of yours.'

Ronan shot her a narrow-eyed stare. 'Why?'

'You must make a fortune for them with your books.'

'They do okay.'

Judging by the dangerously flat-toned edge to his voice, she was onto something. So she calmly crossed her legs beneath the deep russet satin skirt of her new halter-necked evening dress, plucking an imaginary strand of hair off it while she continued.

'Well, they must think so to fork out this amount of money so you can indulge a virgin traveller…'

Apparently she wasn't fooling him with her calm exterior.

'Is this a glimpse of Kerry Doyle from Doyle's of Dublin I'm getting right now?' He jerked his chin at her. 'Because if that's who I'm talking to I'm not sure I like her all that much.'

It stung. But she recognized it for what it was and called him on it. *'Defensive.'*

'You've been weird ever since we got here.'

'Pot. Meet kettle.'

He shrugged his wide shoulders beneath the dinner jacket that had magically appeared out of nowhere. And Kerry was no fool when it came to clothes—she'd recognized it for what it was the second she'd stopped drooling at the sight of him in it. And what it was was expensive. It was as if he'd transformed from her lovably incorrigible rogue to the kind of man who frequented her family's hotel on a regular basis in the blink of an eye. And, added to the lavish surroundings and his ease within them, it had left her wondering who exactly it was she'd fallen for.

When he turned his head and focussed on the pianist she took a deep breath. 'So what does something like this go down as on your expenses sheet?'

'Travel.'

'And that suit you look so gorgeous in?'

'Clothing, funnily enough—glad you approve.'

It was how someone who was dating a secret agent probably felt. 'If you're paying for this entire trip out of your own pocket, then I want to know. And I want to split it with you. It's not like I hadn't already budgeted for it.'

'You're helping me with research for a book.'

It hadn't felt as if she was helping him all that much with a book, actually. Not really. Yes, they'd discussed it, and, yes, he'd spent the very odd occasion on his laptop, but even so…

And now she had a sneaking suspicion there was more to it. *'Ronan—'*

'Kerry—' he looked her straight in the eye, a muscle in his jaw clenching, '—leave it alone. The expenses are taken care of in exchange for the insight I've got from you on travelling for the first time. That was the deal, remember? And I've got more from this trip than you might think I have.'

Oh, he was hard work all right.

She damped her lips, took a sip of her wine and tried a different approach. 'We've never talked much about your family.'

'We've talked plenty about my family.'

Then why was he so defensive about them all of a sudden too? It was as if she were talking to someone she'd never met before!

'I'd like to know more.'

'Why?'

'Possibly because I'm sitting over here feeling like I don't know you as well as I thought I did?'

'Why do you need to know more than you already do?'

Because I'm in love with you and I want to know everything about you. But she couldn't say that, could she? Especially not when he was making her feel as if she'd fallen in love with a fantasy—ironically, when he'd wanted to fulfil all of those...

'What's changed between Fiji and here?'

'Nothing.'

And now he was lying to her? She shook her head, suddenly tired beyond belief—and she couldn't be patient with him when she was tired.

'Do you want out?'

Ronan looked stunned by the question. 'Out?'

She waved a hand back and forth between them. 'Of this. Part of the deal was if either one of us wanted out at any stage we'd go our separate ways, remember?'

'I don't want out.' And he said it with enough controlled anger in his voice for her to know he meant it. 'Do *you*?'

'No. I don't want to argue with you either.'

'Then don't.'

It was tough not to when he was being the way he was. 'You're shutting me out—but you know that, don't you?'

The muscle in his jaw clenched again. He knew. But he wasn't going to stop doing it any time soon, was he? So she might have to give up, temporarily, because this wasn't getting them anywhere—was doing more harm than good to her vulnerable heart.

So she set her glass to one side and, with another deep breath, pushed to her feet. 'I'm going to turn in.'

Ronan frowned up at her as she stepped over, bending down to kiss his cleanly shaven cheek before lowering her voice to add, 'Maybe tomorrow the Ronan I know will come back. I miss him.'

THERE WERE no words to describe how he'd felt when she'd asked him if he wanted 'out'. Angry didn't begin to describe it. Furious wasn't anywhere near *angry* enough. Livid was closer, he supposed. Livid that she'd thought he could just up and walk away from her when they'd only just left the island and all that had happened there. Didn't she have any idea what it was going to take to walk in a few weeks' time—what it was going to take getting through the lead in to it? Why would he try to speed up the process?

But none of that mattered when compared to the moment of panic he'd felt when he'd thought *she* wanted 'out'. And the fact he'd felt it so strongly just went to prove how weak he was when it came to her.

He should have hated her for that.

But instead he was on his way to find her for more damage control. Because any steps he'd tried to introduce it had just blown up in his face. So now he had to try and fix it. And then think up another way of gently backing off so he didn't hurt her any more than he had to.

The narrow corridors of the train weren't as well lit as he'd expected, disorienting him for a moment and forcing him—*godamn it*—to ask for help from a steward, which didn't improve his mood even if it did make him thankful she'd left when she had. And between that and his sudden sense of urgency to get to her it ended up taking longer than he'd planned. Especially when he had to stand outside her door and breathe deeply before he faced her again.

She radiated surprise when she opened the door. He could feel it in the air.

'I *am* the publisher.' He frowned hard when no amount of concentrating would bring her face into focus. Not that he needed to see it to know what she looked like. She was indelibly imprinted onto his brain now—both visually and by touch. But not seeing her—*hurt*—and he didn't want it to.

'Okay.'

He clenched his jaw, shoving his hands deep into his pockets so he wouldn't be tempted to just reach forward, haul her into his arms and kiss it better. 'That's why there's never a problem with expenses.'

'I see.'

He clenched his jaw harder at the words she'd chosen. But he deserved the coolness he was getting, didn't he? If he'd been her he'd probably have slammed the door in his face. 'We own newspapers, magazines and radio stations up and down the country as well.'

'Anything else?'

'Bought into a TV station—that's why I was home.'

'Name?'

'TV station or the company?'

'Actually I was checking yours is still the same but the company name might be interesting too.' She stepped back, letting a little light in. 'Are you coming in?'

No, coming in was a bad idea. It had been tough enough

looking at her in the dress she'd bought. He'd even wondered if she'd bought it specifically to make him crazy. It highlighted the russet in her brown eyes, baring, not just her shoulders, but the most tempting expanse of smooth-skinned back he'd ever set eyes on—and as to how it hugged her curves and dipped between her breasts…

The woman was hotter than Hades.

The door clicked shut behind him and he frowned all the harder, focussing his annoyance at having stepped inside on his other frustration. 'Don't the lights work in here?'

'The little one by the bed is fine.'

The hell it was. Everything was still shadowed and it left him floundering—which he hated to the pit of his stomach. In better light he'd feel as if he was on surer ground. He wanted to be able to see her face while he talked to her so he could gauge her reactions, watch the thoughts as they crossed her expressive eyes.

He wanted to be able to look at her. It was like having his gut put through a mangle.

Kerry's sultry scent surrounded him as she walked past and sat on the edge of what he assumed was the aforementioned bed, the material of her dress rustling, her voice as soft as silk. 'So you're disgustingly rich, then, I take it?'

'Indecently rich—less attractive to you now, am I?'

She ignored the bitterness in his voice. 'So you being some kind of millionaire—it's a secret, is it?'

'Not at home, it's not.'

'But you don't make that big a deal of it when you're away. You like to be accepted as yourself and not because of how much money you have.'

Sometimes he could swear she saw inside him. It was more than a little unnerving—and she didn't wait for him to speak, which meant she already knew the answer.

'What did you say the company was called again?'

He hadn't. 'The Millennium Group.'

'You're *that* O'Keefe?' She laughed huskily. 'Well, now, that *is* interesting.'

The laugh dragged him physically across the room where he exhaled with relief as the lamp shone enough soft light on her face for him to see her, his voice dropping to a calmer tone. 'Interesting how?'

'Because if your father is Brian O'Keefe, then I think he plays golf with my father from time to time.'

Ronan sat down on the deep bed beside her. 'I did wonder how we'd not met when I realized who you were.'

'Not so small a world after all, then.'

'Apparently not.' He took a hand out of his pocket and lifted one of hers from her lap, tangling fingers and resting their joined hands on his thigh, his gaze fixed on the sight. 'I'm not home much—probably explains it some.'

'How do you manage that with such a huge company?'

She sounded genuinely interested in the logistics, which made sense when Ronan thought about it. If she wanted to travel more then she'd need to know how to arrange her working life better. And that was something else he could pass on, wasn't it? He smiled.

'I'm a wizard when it comes to the art of delegation. Surround yourself with good people, reward them for good work and you get people you can trust.' It was just that simple, he'd found. 'Doesn't matter if it's a big company with dozens of divisions or an iconic hotel in the middle of Dublin—it's all about teamwork.'

'You make it sound easy.'

And the edge of wistfulness in her voice practically crucified him, his gaze shifting to hold hers. 'It is. You just have to be determined to make it work. And be prepared to weather the odd muck-up from time to time.'

She grimaced and Ronan smiled affectionately, his free

hand reaching to tuck a lock of soft hair behind her ear, fingertips tracing her long droplet earring on the way down so his knuckles grazed the sensitive skin on her neck. 'You can let go a little if you put your mind to it. If you want something badly enough you work towards it—and I'll bet you're great with goals.'

'Is that why you're in here making up with me after our first real argument?'

'We didn't argue.'

'We did—we just did it *very quietly* this time. It's the silent ones do the most damage,' And she lowered her voice to a stage whisper as if it were some kind of secret or maybe in case someone somewhere heard her and proved her wrong later on by making a loud argument do the most damage.

It would happen in some version at some point and Ronan knew that, his voice rough with the knowledge. 'You can do it, you know—delegate more so you can travel to all the places you want to. Think about it.'

Kerry smiled a smile that tipped the lid off his sanity. 'I will.'

She was beautiful. In sunlight she glowed, when she laughed she lit up from inside—but in soft lamplight that made the sparkling in her eyes look like stardust she was breathtakingly beautiful. And that was *exactly* what she was doing to him: stealing his breath—making his lungs ache for its loss—his heart thundering so hard in his chest he could barely hear the sound of the train running over the tracks below them.

He suddenly couldn't speak.

Kerry searched his eyes for the longest time, the backs of her fine-boned fingers still resting softly against his thigh and her free hand lifting to frame his face as she smiled the softest, most sensual smile he'd ever seen.

But she didn't say anything.

Instead she let her hand gently turn his face before sliding over his jaw and round to the nape of his neck where she added enough pressure to close the gap between them—her chin lifting so she could press her full, soft, warm lips to his.

Need flashed through him like a firework exploding in the sky—the point of detonation dead centre in his chest and radiating outwards in a shower of burning sprinkles until his skin tingled from the scalp on top of his head to the very soles of his feet.

Dear God, how was he supposed to leave this woman? Give him strength.

'*Stay.*' The word was said against his lips.

Ronan was a weak man.

CHAPTER NINE

THE woman who'd left Ireland wasn't the same one who'd return. Kerry smiled at the thought.

The train travelled north where they disembarked for a private visit to a Hunter Valley vineyard and cellar in Australia's wine-growing region—Kerry still drunk enough from the memories of a night with Ronan to not feel any great effects from the wine-tasting. Then they made their way towards Brisbane—spending a day and a half exploring the city and two nights exploring each other. And on the fifth day they stayed on the train while it passed through the scenery of rural Queensland—laughing over lunch, kissing on the observation deck of one of the carriages, retiring early to their cabin; *theirs* because the other one had become a tad redundant...

Day six was a wondrous adventure to discover the Great Barrier Reef—they were flown onto a private pontoon to swim, snorkel and discover yet more amazing marine life, Ronan then ordering fish for lunch just to tease out her sense of moral outrage at him eating something they'd spent all morning admiring.

'How could you?' She laughed. *'Murderer.'*

And before the trip ended they ascended the scenic MacAlister Range to Kuranda to take a breathtaking cable-car ride above the rainforest treetops where Kerry got so emotional about the beauty of it she almost wept.

'Oh, no, you don't.' Ronan drew her into his arms. 'We talked about this in Fiji…'

So she tried to explain 'happy tears' to him between the kisses he plied her with to 'make her feel better'. But he said he wasn't buying that—and continued making his point about feeling better with admirable displays of diligence and attention to detail in their cabin practically the whole way back to Sydney…

Kerry had left home with a starry-eyed dream of seeing the world and was approaching the homeward journey feeling a bit as if she'd had it handed to her.

It was just that simple.

But she still hadn't said the words. Thing was, even at her age, she'd never once been in a situation where her heart and soul were on the line—not to the same extent as they were now. She was so very, very happy but she knew the universe had an unerring habit of balancing the good things with equal measures of bad.

Loving Ronan the way she did, it therefore followed that the balance of life could very well break her into billions of irreparable pieces if she had to give him up. But she had spent too much of her life being cautious to hold anything back now.

When he would look at her with so much quiet intensity, touch her every chance he got, smile at her with so much warmth, it convinced her she was cared for in return. That if they could just find the courage to take a chance they might find a way to make it work.

'I hope whatever it is you went to get was worth the embarrassment of almost single-handedly demolishing that poor man's shop displays.' She smiled impishly at him from the bench she'd been ordered not to leave 'til he got back.

Ronan frowned. 'I thought we agreed no peeking?'

'The crashing sound followed by lots of shouting in Chinese kinda caught my attention.'

He plunked himself down on the bench beside her, tossing a bag onto her lap with a dramatic sigh. 'See, that's what I get for trying to do something nice. Did it ever occur to you, young lady, that part of the reason I don't do it more often is 'cos you're so un-flipping-appreciative of my efforts?'

Kerry spluttered. 'I think you'll find I've been nothing *but* appreciative of your *many* efforts for quite some time now. Do I need to up my game?'

Absent-mindedly scratching his chest, Ronan studied the orderly chaos of Hong Kong around them: clanging trams festooned with unfathomable Chinese advertisements, buses careering round corners and parting scurrying crowds. 'If you up your game any I think you might kill me.'

He flashed a devilishly sexy smile and Kerry grinned in return. Lord, but she had it bad.

A nod was aimed at the bag. 'Go on, then.'

Any notion she might have had about teasing him again died an immediate death when she looked in it; wide eyes blinking with surprise while a lump of emotion clogged her throat.

When she didn't speak he leaned forwards to study her face. 'Wrong type of stuff?'

Kerry shook her head, her lower lip trembling. 'No.'

He lifted his hand to tug on the end of her pony-tail, his deep voice threaded with the gentleness that always made her heart shift. 'Figured you could make some souvenirs of your own so you don't go mental with the shopping again.'

Oh, he could try and make jokes about this one. But what he'd done was the most amazingly considerate, thoughtful, caring, romantic—

He had *no* idea how deeply it touched her.

'Tell me you're not about to cry?' With a low chuckle he jerked his brows. 'Didn't we have this discussion above a rainforest? Don't make me use the same tactic all over again now.'

She almost choked letting a burst of laughter out, because

if that'd been meant as a threat it was hardly likely to be effective, was it?

'I love that you thought of this.'

He shrugged it off. 'Paint me something pretty to keep when we're done and we'll be even.'

'When we're done'. The flash of pain when he said the words so calmly was swift. He had a tendency to drop them into conversation at random. Never seeming to see the damage they did.

But, Kerry being Kerry, she did what she always did when he inadvertently reminded her they still hadn't talked about the possibility of seeing each other when the trip was over. She tried to get closer; it was a knee-jerk reaction.

Setting the bag of art material to one side, she climbed over onto his lap—his hands automatically rising to her waist and the sound of a familiar deep chuckle vibrating between them before she silenced him with a long, slow kiss. His large hands flexed tighter, he hummed against her lips and Kerry smiled inside, threading her fingers into his short hair.

Then she rained kisses all over his gorgeous face.

Ronan laughed throatily. 'Would you quit it, woman? You'll wear me out before we get to Dubai.'

But when she kissed him again he didn't protest, instead making a pretty good job of wearing *her* out by kissing her back until she saw stars behind her eyes. Only when she was breathless and languid and lying across his lap with her head on his shoulder and his arm for support did he reach for the bag again and drop it on her, planting a kiss on her forehead before hoisting her up and setting her on her feet.

'I think you should paint me a temple first.'

Kerry held the top edge of the bag in both hands, a small frown on her face. 'It's been a long time since—'

'You'll be rusty, that's all.' He stopped in the middle of the crowd, hands back on her waist to haul her in closer before he bent his knees and ducked down to look up into her eyes. 'You should never give up your dreams, Kerry, Kerry Doyle— you hear? Just because your life changes doesn't mean you give everything else up.'

For someone who didn't want her to cry, he always seemed to do a good job of saying things that choked her up. 'I couldn't paint.'

'You said your tutors said you weren't that bad.'

Kerry hit him in the chest with the bag. 'No, you idiot, not I couldn't as in I was no good—I *couldn't*.'

'Why?'

She shrugged one shoulder.

But that combined with the way she couldn't look him in the eye was enough for Ronan to want to know more, standing tall, his hands lifting from her waist to frame her face before he used the pads of his thumbs below her chin to tilt her head up so he could look her in the eye.

'Tell me.'

When he used the soft tone that always seemed to work best on her, she smiled the smile that always hit him dead centre in his chest. 'You're doing that thing you do again.'

'Which thing?' He puffed his chest out. 'I have a wide and varied repertoire.'

'Oh, I *know*.' She laid the bag against his chest and leaned on it, her eyes darkening and her voice huskily low so he knew her thoughts had just gone exactly where his had. 'You're wheedling information out of me by being sweet and gentle.'

Ronan snorted in disgust. 'Sweet and gentle? What are you trying to do to my reputation?'

Dropping her head towards her shoulder, her pony-tail swinging against his fingers, she quirked her brows. 'I know—the truth hurts.'

Damn but she was amazing. Even when insulting him.

He kissed her as a sweet rebuke, only stopping when she

was leaning into him as if her legs couldn't hold her up. And he loved that he could do that to her, so he smiled.

'Tell me.'

She took a deep breath, her chin dropping so that she was directing her words at the open collar of his shirt. 'I just couldn't. When I painted I was happy. And it just felt wrong, even for a moment, to feel that happy and—I don't know—content, I guess, when everyone else was so lost in grief.'

'So you put all your energy into helping them instead. And buried how you felt while doing it, right?'

She aimed a wry smile at his throat. 'Sometimes it astounds me that you can do that.'

'Do what?'

'Explain me so easily.'

It made him smile. Because he remembered how he'd felt his first day with her, a lifetime ago in New York, when he'd not 'got' her at all—and it had intrigued him. Getting to know Kerry was a gradual process—like peeling back the layers of an onion— and the more he learned and understood, the more he liked what he found. But that was a downward slide, wasn't it?

He just couldn't seem to stop himself from wanting to take that slide, though.

'You always put other people first.'

She frowned. 'You make it sound like a weakness.'

'It is. If you don't keep anything for yourself.' When a look of pain crossed her face—and, yes, he did notice, because she might think she hid them when they happened but she wasn't that good at it—he took a deep breath and tilted her chin back up. 'Which is why you should paint. Make time for it. If it makes you happy you shouldn't *not* do it—*promise me*.'

Kerry searched his eyes for the longest time. And when she did that it always frightened him because she was so very good at seeing inside him. She seemed to know the right moment to tease him, when to smile the soft smile that soothed his soul, when to crawl onto his lap and kiss him until he couldn't think about anything but the here and now…

But it made him fearful of her seeing the one thing he didn't want her to see. Actually, that was a lie—there was more than the one now.

Her voice was seduction personified. 'I promise.'

She looked at him with such intense warmth it was like looking directly into her heart—and that slayed him, tore him in half; half wanting to physically throw her away from him and deny what he saw there by roaring at her and saying things to make her hate him, and the other half wanting to haul her close and throw his head back so he could laugh mani-cally at the sky with joy.

Swallowing down a tsunami of angry regret, he dropped his chin and sought her hand, tangling their fingers before tugging her through the crowd. 'C'mon—I'm sure I saw a temple somewhere.'

It wouldn't be that hard to find one. At every junction there was a different Hong Kong from the chaos they were currently standing in: tiny Taoist temples suffused with incense, plangent bells and beating gongs or an apron of grass where office workers were practising T'ai Chi. And frankly Ronan could do with finding that kind of peace somewhere else when the only time he seemed to truly feel it was when he looked into a pair of autumnal eyes…

He had to stop doing this—to both of them.

No amount of losing himself in the moment was going to change the future.

And if he hadn't felt that way in Hong Kong, then in Dubai he had a big enough reminder thrown straight at him to jerk him back into reality.

He should have known better. But it was what he got for allowing himself to feel so full of male pride at how Kerry reacted to everything he did and everywhere they went. And what was it they said about pride and falling over?

Purposefully he'd headed them for the Creek, the heart of 'old' Dubai. East of the major Jumeirah developments, it was a sea inlet where, between downtown high-rises, some of the area's more venerable traditions still survived—and Ronan had known instinctively Kerry would love it there. Because at the end of the day, the trip had long since been all about what Kerry would love best. He wanted to hand her the world on a silver platter and say, 'Here—it's yours—grab hold of it.'

As if he were handing on an imaginary baton...

And the way her face lit up with enthusiasm was reward enough. She could light up from inside the way she did for ever as far as he was concerned. It was how he planned on re-membering her when he let her go.

Along the wharves of the creek were multi-decked, wooden dhows that'd plied the Gulf for centuries—sailors' laundry flapping as the boats rocked gently at their moorings, the clothes tossed in the same breeze that waved Kerry's rich chestnut hair around her shoulders and into her eyes so that either she, or more often than not Ronan himself, was con-stantly reaching up and tucking it behind her ears.

Next up were walls of cargo they laid bets on the contents of—sacks of basmati rice, boxed electronic goods from Malaysia, fridges from China—while water taxis chugged past them to spirit workers across the water to where a mosque, a Hindu temple and a Sikh gurdwara stood side by side. And on both banks of the estuary, the sight of a grid of souks announcing Dubai's original *raison d'être* was enough of a reason for Kerry to laugh joyously at the combined sights, flinging her arms around his neck and kissing him until he finally admitted to himself she could very easily have been *his raison d'être*...in a different life...given the chance...

He did it again: got lost being with her, blocking out his reality.

The hint of what was to come should have been in the afternoon, when they wandered the narrow streets and covered walkways monopolized by gold, spices, saffron, heady perfume and countless textiles. Kerry marvelled—with the kind of blatant jealousy that made Ronan chuckle under his breath— as women veiled in black clutching expensive handbags peered into shop windows at enough varying wares to appeal to the professional shopper. So he in turn pointed out to her the men in white robes and classic checked headgear strolling, sitting and chatting without the least bit of interest in shopping...

'The world won't end if you don't shop,' he calmly informed her, stifling his need to laugh out loud at her expression.

To which she replied with an elbow in his ribs and a smirk, 'Economies will crash if I don't—trust me.'

But it was those narrow streets that proved his downfall. Because while wandering hand in hand with her he made the mistake of letting time get away from him. And even though at nightfall things came alive with neon signs vying with glittering jewels and the streets thronged with locals and foreigners from pretty much everywhere, the fact remained—*night fell*. So while, with a sickening jolt of realization, he'd known he'd made a serious mistake and had headed sharply back in the direction of the hotel—they'd already walked too far for him to do anything about it getting dark too fast.

He was pretty much stuffed after that.

At first he could have put the constant bumping into people down to the fact the streets were so crowded, but every now and again they would hit a spot that wasn't so well lit up and when they did he froze, turning to try and find something he could latch onto to get him out of trouble—out of the terrible darkness he'd one day all too soon have to live in.

Kerry caught on the second time it happened. 'Are we lost?'

'Hmm?' He frowned hard, narrowing his eyes to try and find a lifeline. Wasn't as if he could tell her if they were, was it? And he'd tell her what was really wrong and ask for her help over his cold, rotting corpse. The steward on the train had been bad enough. But to ask Kerry to be some kind of two-legged guide dog? No chance!

Stupid, stupid, STUPID mistake. He should have paid more attention; shouldn't have let himself get sucked into a bubble of make-believe with her. She'd *made* him forget. And now he was in danger of literally falling flat on his face and ending up looking like the biggest loser of all time.

She laughed and he felt her step closer to his side. 'We're lost, aren't we?'

Fighting down a wave of the kind of frustration he was still fairly new at trying to master, he turned his face to her voice, racking every inch of his brain for a solution. 'Have I ever got us lost, woman?'

'They say there's a first time for everything...'

Ronan's heart was now thundering in his chest and in his ears—which was a pain in the behind when he needed to be able to hear. *Don't panic, Ronan—deep breaths—keep smiling—find something to aim for.* That was the plan so far. And at least with her hand held in his he only had the one arm to keep from doing something really pathetic like wavering out in front of his body. God, how much he *hated this*.

And now she was chuckling.

Damping down the need to rage at her for something that wasn't her fault, he gritted his teeth and threw out an option. 'Okay, then—you're such a well-seasoned traveller now, you get us back to the hotel. I'll let you lead the way.'

'Oh, my—the *pressure*...'

'Yup—and I have that much faith in my training I'm even going to close my eyes 'til we get there.'

'So you're *completely* in my hands, are you?'

'Let's even that up some, shall we?' Using the hand he held, he tugged her towards him, moving the backs of his fingers until he got his bearings so he could place both hands on her waist. And the sound of her husky laughter while he closed his eyes and made a game out of running his hands over her body was enough to give him faith in the fact he was getting away with it—in more ways than one.

He turned her round, wrapped his arms around her waist and lowered his head to her hair—breathing a deep breath of her amazing scent before placing his cheek against her ear to grumble, 'Now—back to the hotel so I can be completely in your hands *properly*.'

Her hands lifted to lie on his at her waist as she started walking. 'Still incorrigible, you know.'

And a genius.

Because not only had he just got himself out of the danger zone, he had her in his arms and was able to nuzzle her neck and mumble in her ear at the same time.

'You love that I'm incorrigible.'

Kerry laughed again, guiding them through the crowd. 'I kinda do.'

'What can I say? I'm a lovable kinda guy.'

'You have your moments.'

'I'm the best travel guide you've ever had—*face it*.' He managed to get his thumbs under the edge of her cotton top, smoothing over warm, soft skin above the waistband of her linen trousers.

'You're the *only* travel guide I've ever had—and you *know that*.' She mirrored the movements of his thumbs on the backs of his hands, her voice full of a smile when she moved to one side and he stumbled. 'You still have your eyes closed, don't you, you idiot?'

'I do.' He took a deep breath of Kerry-scented air and opened his eyes. 'Can't see a thing.'

Nothing. Just blackness; that all-engulfing fall down a bottomless hole into nothingness—and he wasn't somewhere where he knew how many steps to count to get to somewhere, which meant it was tough to damp down the rising bubble of panic in his stomach that made him nauseous. And it was that natural need to panic that did his head in most, because it was a sign of fear. It led him to think about the awful sense of loneliness he'd felt the first time he'd ignored the deep-seated need to switch on every light he could find, instead forcing himself to sit in the dark, facing his fear—facing his future. Then he'd gone through the inevitable stage of chasing every option there might be in the known universe, no matter where or what the cost was or how experimental. And now he was at the end of the line.

He couldn't hide from it, couldn't outrun it. Couldn't play let's pretend with Kerry for ever…no matter how much he wanted to…

'You're still insane…'

Breathing deep to ease the pain in his chest, he played along. 'Insanity is a large part of my charm. That's why dozens of women chat me up on planes and end up falling for the "let me give you the world" line…'

Her shoulders shook against his chest. 'If I *had* fallen for that line women all over the planet would be making feminist pilgrimages to my house to beat me to death. That's not what I fell for.'

The words were immediately followed by a tensing in her slight frame and Ronan felt it, frowning hard in response. He was officially an ass. Leading her down a path where he might trick her into saying the words he'd have wanted to hear more than anything else in another life was cruel. Hell, she might not even feel them. And if he hadn't been so selfish he wouldn't have wanted her to. But he did.

God, how much he wanted he wanted to hear them.

When his chest constricted enough to cause him actual physical pain, he tightened his arms around her waist—as if subliminally trying to hold on, frowning all the harder when he realized what he'd done. Enough was enough. And this little reminder had been sent to tell him that.

So he dug down deep inside for the words to start pushing her away. He'd managed a few before but they'd been half-hearted efforts. It was time to up his game.

'Well, then, I'd better think up a new line for the next woman who chats me up on a plane, hadn't I? Now that I know how much fun it can be playing tour guide it seems a shame not to do it again. I might try for a blonde next time, though—you know, for variety…'

He felt the sharp intake of breath through the arms around her waist, inwardly cursing the universe when he closed his eyes again.

'A girl on every continent, huh?'

Credit where credit was due—she managed to keep her voice light—and it wasn't as if he could see the flash of pain in her eyes or whispering over her face.

It was the first time he'd ever been thankful for that kind of blessing in disguise.

'Suits the lifestyle of a rolling stone, don't you think?' And if she even for one second thought about suggesting she fill the post of 'Irish-girl-for-every-continent' she'd give him the perfect opportunity to start a massive row. If any man *dared* treat Kerry like that Ronan would—

Would what? He couldn't have it both ways, could he? But it would be an icy day in hell when he'd let her sell herself short like that.

'No home and hearth for Ronan Indiana Jones O'Keefe in this lifetime, then, I take it?'

He hesitated on an answer, took time to swallow down the bitter burst of laughter generated by her cool words. For a moment he allowed himself to look down into the dark pit of his soul that was filled with raw emotion and self-pity.

Residual bitterness laced his voice as a result. 'May as well just put me in a box.'

Kerry Doyle was the right woman in the right place at the wrong time, he told himself. That was all. *And it killed him.*

He forced a smile onto his face. 'Are we there yet?'

'If you start asking me that every five minutes, Ronan, I swear—'

'Are we there yet?'

CHAPTER TEN

PARIS in the autumn. It was an amazing way to end their trip—would have been nigh on perfect if it hadn't included the word 'end'.

And the fact they hadn't even broached the subject of seeing each other ever again was making Kerry ache every single second of every day. Since Dubai it had mushroomed until it felt like a cloud constantly hanging over her head. And Ronan had been dropping more and more of his deeply hurtful, supposed-to-be-flippant statements out into the air since Dubai too, which didn't exactly give her the confidence to search for a possible solution.

Thing was, for every one of the things he said that she found painful, he did a half-dozen things that made her believe he cared for her more than he was letting on. When he'd talked about other women he'd held onto her so tightly it was as if he never wanted to let go. When he'd talk about any future trips she could take alone he'd spent a long time making quite sure she wouldn't visit anywhere she might be placed in harm's way—with ad-libbed warnings about talking to 'handsome strangers' on planes or anywhere else for that matter, as if the idea would bug him even when he wasn't there. And then there was the way he would make love to her…

Making her believe she was deeply loved, as if she was

the most precious woman in the world; one he would never, ever tire of.

How could he do that if he didn't care?

When she'd told him she had to be at the Jardin du Luxembourg on the fifth because she'd made a promise to Nana, he'd booked them into a hotel in the traditionally intellectual heart of the city. And, like everywhere he'd ever taken her, it was perfect. South of Île de la Cité—she could almost feel the ghosts of long-ago writers, philosophers and jazz legends haunting the cafés and nightspots all around them.

And then, to add to the list of positive signs Kerry was almost desperately forming, he took her straight to the Musée d'Orsay—reputedly one of the best spaces to enjoy art in the world. The building itself was enough to convince Kerry—it was a light-filled work of iron, glass and moulded plaster with windows fit for a cathedral, barring the lack of coloured glass. It was gorgeous, the bright light lifting her spirits and letting her dare to hope for a solution again.

And Kerry loved that he was so keen to make sure she renewed her interest in art. Heaven knew he'd sat over her shoulder enough times when she'd started painting again in Hong Kong, until she'd finally given up and admitted she couldn't concentrate with him being there—for *varying* reasons. But he'd always wanted to see what she'd done, had been impressed just the right amount for her to know he'd genuinely meant it and, after spending many an hour patiently tapping away on his laptop or reading while she'd sketched and painted, he'd taken a lot of time choosing which ones he wanted to keep.

Would he really have done that if he hadn't cared?

They spent the entire morning meandering through the galleries distributed on either side of the central nave, paying special attention to a collection of impressionist and post-impressionist paintings by the greats. Monet, Degas, Renoir,

Cézanne, Van Gogh, Gauguin, Seurat, Pissarro… The names were never-ending. It really couldn't get much better, except there was a 'something'—something just not quite *right*.

Then it hit her. It was how Ronan was studying things.

She didn't know what it was about the way he looked at everything but it was somehow—odd—to her after a while; a little *too* intense, maybe? Not that she didn't appreciate him trying to make the effort for her, but there was just… *something*…

Near the end of the impressionist paintings she caught him pinching then rubbing the bridge of his nose between his thumb and forefinger.

'Headache?' Well, that would make sense of it.

Ronan turned his head to look at her, blinking a couple of times as her question sank in. 'No, why?'

'You're pinching your nose the way people do when they have a headache.'

The smile took a split second to land on the sinful mouth she loved so much. 'I'm not used to staring at these things, is all. They're starting to blur together.'

Kerry would have bought that if there hadn't been that split second of hesitation before he smiled. She was a connoisseur of his smiles, after all. And of the varying sexy, slow, lazy, cheeky or even bemused smiles he had—not one of them had ever been hesitant about making an appearance.

She narrowed her eyes and studied him.

Ronan frowned, then stepped forwards and took her elbow. 'Well, I don't know about you but all this art appreciation has my stomach rumbling.'

When she resisted the gentle tug he looked down at her, his brows sliding up a quarter-inch in question. But when she tilted her head and studied each of his stunning eyes in turn he frowned harder.

'What?'

'Are you sure you're okay?' Her mind found another viable reason for what it might be. 'You really didn't have to spend all morning wandering round here if it's not your cup of tea, you know. I'd have been happy wherever we went. Aren't I always?'

'I thought you'd enjoy it.' He shrugged.

She smiled. 'I have.'

'Well, then.'

The second time he tugged she followed. But when he turned he practically knocked over a tourist with a video camera. Immediately releasing her elbow, he caught the small woman's arms to stop her from falling.

'Excusez moi, mademoiselle.'

One of his patented smiles was enough to earn forgiveness—and the immediate arrival of a man who proved the woman was a 'madame' rather than a 'mademoiselle'. And then Ronan stood tall, turning his head before a slow smile appeared as he reached for Kerry again.

'Low blood sugar. Need. Food. Now.'

Kerry smiled as she shook her head, but the whole way down the stairs with her hand grasped firmly in his she couldn't help but feel the oppressive weight of the 'something not quite right' sitting on her shoulders. And it made her stare all the harder at him, which in turn led her to notice things she hadn't noticed before.

Such as how he was constantly turning his head to look around him.

It had always been one of the things she loved about him—the way he would take everything in. She'd known from the beginning that he was highly intelligent and if his quick wit hadn't hinted at it then his vast stored knowledge of everywhere they went would. So she'd always put his quiet intensity down to intelligence. But something wasn't right.

What was it?

'Do you want anything from the gift shop?'

And now he was inviting her to shop? There was something very wrong.

'I might get some postcards of the paintings we saw.' She pursed her lips and pushed to see just how distracted he was by whatever it was. 'Maybe some T-shirts or a framed print or any history of art books they have that look any good…'

'Okay.' He turned his head and studied the shop for a second, releasing her elbow. 'I'm gonna get some fresh air— I'll meet you by the river.'

'Okay.' But she didn't move, her feet rooted to the floor while she watched his tall frame striding with familiar confident ease along the brightly lit arched thoroughfare and out the doors into bright sunshine.

And she still didn't move.

Lifting her hands to her jean-clad hips, she blinked hard as she focussed on a random spot in the middle of the glorious windows curving up into the ceiling, trying to force her brain to remember any other times when he'd done anything that might have been considered 'odd' if she hadn't been so distracted by other things. That was the problem, though—he'd been thoroughly distracting from the very beginning. And that, coupled with the many amazing places they'd been to and the cornucopia of emotions that battled and then blossomed as their journey progressed, had been more than enough to keep her mind occupied.

Maybe she was overreacting? So desperate to grab at straws that might indicate he cared anywhere near as much as she did, so aware of the sand slipping inexorably through the hourglass measuring their time together…

She shook her head, inwardly berating herself for being plain old daft. The man had a headache and was being a baby about it—full stop.

* * *

Ronan watched the water lapping against the banks of the Seine, then tipped his head back to look up at the bright blue sky above him, filling his lungs with crisp air to try and clear his head. He had the headache from hell. Though why he couldn't have just said that to Kerry he had no idea—male pride, no doubt—but had he really got that touchy about any sign of weakness? How pathetic did that make him?

And then he'd practically steamrollered over some poor unsuspecting tourist. *In front of Kerry.*

Maybe it was just as well they were almost done.

Even if every cell in his body felt as if it were shrivelling up and dying at the very thought of it.

Instead of standing feeling sorry for himself he should really have a think about how exactly he was going to distance himself from her over the next few days. Because so far any of the ideas he'd had had turned his stomach. Flirting with another woman under her nose would be plain low and he didn't think he could do it with any great level of conviction anyway. Picking a fight was an option, but then that meant he'd have to stand there looking into her eyes and seeing the very second he started hurting her. And he knew he'd have a difficult job not giving in to the need to make it better if that happened.

That left physically distancing himself some more. He could suggest splitting up for the afternoon—that would be a start. And there were a few people he could drop in on and tick off his list. He just needed to make sure there wasn't the tiniest sliver of a chance of Kerry talking about meeting up again in the future…

The sound of a boat engine got him to drop his chin long enough to watch as it went by—allowing himself to surrender to an overwhelming sense of emptiness as he did. And then he had a go at seeing how much he could see on the opposite river bank while he rehearsed what he'd say in his head—each word already tasting like acid on the back of his tongue.

Kerry smiled when she saw him. There was just something about the sight of a gorgeous male on an autumn day standing by the banks of the Seine with the wind catching the edge of his chocolate cord jacket and a frame of chestnuts, poplars and maples in hundreds of shades fit for the paintings they'd spent a morning looking at over his head, leaves billowing down and scattering at his feet…

She moved the box of headache tablets she'd found in the bottom of her bag end over end in her hand as she approached him. And was less than twenty yards away when she slowed down.

Random memories suddenly flashed into her head in such a jumble it took a second for her to try and sort through them. She was being daft again, wasn't she? So she shook her head yet again and stepped forwards—her gaze locked on Ronan's profile.

Lifting a hand, she waved at him.

A couple of steps closer and for no reason in the world she could feel a lump forming in her throat. He was still staring straight ahead, so she looked to see what it was that had his attention so fully he wasn't catching a glimpse of her from his peripheral vision. She had on a long bright red sweater, after all, so you'd have thought he'd have noticed…

A couple of feet away, steps faltering, she held her breath, waved again—and still got nothing. Completely out of the blue it made her think about the time she'd waved like an idiot at him in front of the Empire State Building and he hadn't noticed then either…

He turned his face towards her and smiled. 'Creeping up on me to go "boo", were we? I didn't see you.'

And just like that, instinctively, she knew. With a throw-away phrase millions of people all over the world probably used every day, Kerry's female intuition kicked in and she *knew*. Knew but didn't want to know—every part of her willing it not to be.

'You didn't see me.'

Ronan frowned at the monotone in her voice, stepping forwards when he saw what must have been written all over her face. 'What's wrong?'

Kerry stared back at him, her chin lifting as he closed the last of the gap. 'You couldn't see me. Because you have no peripheral vision, do you?'

From the very beginning he'd never once looked sideways at her, had he? He always turned his head or moved his upper body—and then there were all the times he'd bumped into things…

He let out a huff of air that made a feeble attempt at being laughter, and she could practically see the lies formulating. 'Where did that come from?'

Not lies, then—she'd been wrong about that. Not the truth or an answer—but *not a denial*. Damn her stupid intuition. And the 'something not quite right' was sitting so heavily on her chest she could barely breathe while her mind filled in some of the clues: elbowing her on the plane, jostling people in crowds in New York, the displays he'd knocked over in Hong Kong and the tiny woman he'd almost flattened not that long ago when he'd turned too fast.

Ronan was holding himself taller, was breathing a little faster, smiling a smile that didn't make it up into his eyes, his stunning, beautiful eyes—the eyes that had been the first thing she'd fallen for.

'You have no peripheral vision.' She said it again so he'd know she knew. And maybe because she needed to repeat things to make her heart believe them when it ached not to. 'How bad is it? How much can you—'

Oh, dear God. Her mouth went dry as she pieced together a little more, her breathing now a series of short, sharp breaths that put her about two minutes away from the very first panic attack of her life.

'*Dubai*—' She choked on the word and had to clear her throat before trying again, her eyes misting. 'In Dubai…you couldn't…that night…you couldn't…'

'Kerry—'

No, she had to keep going now she'd started; she had to know all of it. 'You c-couldn't see in the dark, could you? You made it…into a game…but—'

'*Stop.*'

His whole expression changed, his face literally darkening. He was angry she'd figured it out? He hadn't intended to tell her, had he? All that time he'd been fighting the need to kiss her, to want her—particularly in Fiji—it was because he didn't want to take a chance on her finding out. Whereas in New York that first time it hadn't mattered, because there was no chance of her figuring it out in one day…

It killed her.

'You couldn't *see*, could you?'

He shifted his weight from one foot to the other, frowning harder, a muscle in his jaw clenched and then finally she got a calm, completely monotone, 'No.'

How had she not known? Why hadn't she caught it? All those times they'd had dinner in well-lit streets and restaurants, all the times he'd arranged morning flights so they went to sleep early. But in Dubai he'd made a mistake, hadn't he? After being so careful to hide it for so long he must have lost track of time; darkness had crept in and he'd held her hand tighter and walked faster to try to get to somewhere he could hide it from her again. And when they'd walked out of any light—he'd stopped and turned round and—and she'd thought he was *lost*. She felt as if she'd been hit by a bus.

He'd been so *devious*. 'Night blindness.'

'Yes.'

'And in the daylight?'

'Tunnel vision.'

He was so deathly calm, so matter-of-fact, while Kerry couldn't breathe any more, she genuinely couldn't. And she was suddenly cold—the shivering starting deep inside and radiating out until she could feel it in her bones and her teeth threatened to chatter.

Ronan reached his hands up but she automatically stepped back—because if he held her she'd crumble.

His voice was full of barely suppressed anger at the small movement. 'Quit it, Kerry. I mean it—you're working yourself up into a state over—'

'Nothing?' She laughed a little hysterically. 'Don't you dare say it's nothing! How bad is it?'

'Kerry—'

'How bad?' Her voice cracked on the words one octave away from being yelled at him.

And the simple answer broke her.

'Progressive.'

She literally folded, bending a little at the waist to try and get her breathing under control as a low moan escaped her lips. *Not him.* Not Ronan. He spent his life seeing all those wondrous places—travelling the world and collecting a million moments he could store in his memory. *Seeing them was his life.* And he was losing that? *No!* She wanted to wail at the unfairness of it.

All the places he'd shown her; places so magical and wonderful and beautiful and he wouldn't be able to see them again? How could he stand it? How could he be so calm about it? How—

'Come on.' His large hands grasped hold of her arms to draw her forwards, voice back to a low monotone again. 'Let's sit you down. And you know how I feel about crying, so you need to stop.'

'Don't cry—not because of me—you hear?' Words said to her in the dark when he'd held her in his arms in the four-poster bed that first time she'd cried. *Not because of him* he'd said. He'd told her he could see her in the dark; had traced her face with his fingertips as if he was memorizing her.

She was dying inside.

And when she lifted her chin to look at him she didn't make any attempt to hide the tears streaming down her face. So many signs all along the way and she'd missed every single one of them.

Ronan took one look at her and swore viciously under his breath, his fingers tightening. 'This is *exactly* why I wasn't ever telling you. I won't have you looking at me like I'm a flipping injured puppy! And I sure won't have you doing this in front of me. You think I *need* this from you?'

'You can't tell me not to be upset about this, Ronan—how can I *not* be? It's *you*.' She tugged her arms free so she could swipe angrily at her cheeks. 'Your whole life revolves around seeing things. How can you—?'

She froze when another piece of the puzzle dropped into place, her gaze locking on a pulse beating in the tight line of his neck and then rising, slowly, until she was looking into the eyes she loved.

'You've been saying goodbye to everyone, haven't you? All those people you've met up with everywhere we've been—*dear God*.' She swallowed hard. 'Frank and Abbie. That's why they were so upset—they *know*. They walked us down the beach every night so I wouldn't know you couldn't see in the dark, didn't they? And you wouldn't throw your garland out the—you wouldn't because you *knew*—'

He knew he wasn't going back? And he'd let her throw hers out the window and they'd watched together as it floated back to shore. She felt so betrayed; as if she'd been the last one on the planet to know. They'd *all* kept it from her.

The moan building inside her made her wrap her arms around her waist to hold it in while the tears formed heated rivers on her cheeks.

'*And me*. This trip with me.' She flung a listless arm out to one side and returned it to her waist, her gaze dropping to the base of his throat again because it hurt too much to look in his eyes while she laid it all out. 'You're what? *Grooming me?* All those times we've talked about places you think I should see—all the places you took me to—to make me fall in love with travelling. And the travelling light lesson and the virgin traveller learning from the pro…'

A sob broke free. 'Talking to me…about *delegating*. So I could make more time to travel.'

When she'd thought at the time he might have been hinting if she made more time they might be able to travel together again…

'*Just because your life changes doesn't mean you give everything else up*.' That was what he'd said to her about her painting that day.

But all along he'd been handing some kind of imaginary baton on to her while he said goodbye to all the friends he'd made over the years, because he—

Because he was locking *everyone* out?

Her eyes rose. 'This is your last trip.'

After he'd said *that* to *her*? He was going to what, then? Relegate himself to half a life? Shut the world out and go home and never see any of the friends he'd made again? He thought because he wouldn't be able to see their faces it meant he should never visit them again? Didn't he know how much his friends loved him? She'd seen him with Frank and Abbie, for crying out loud! How could he think that they'd never want to see him again? How could he lock himself away?

'May as well just put me in a box.'

She sobbed again. Damn it—*he'd said that himself!* How could such an intelligent man be so incredibly dumb? How? And he'd said it with so much derision in his voice she'd believed he was telling her it was a fate worse than death to be at home in Ireland. She'd thought he was telling her that someone like him would never settle down—that she shouldn't think he might want to be tied down by her in any way. And he'd been dropping all those things into conversations ever since—pushing her away, little by little. She'd thought it was because he didn't care as much as she did.

No, that wasn't right. She'd made a complete fool of herself by making a pass at him only to be turned down, and then she'd thought he didn't want her the same way she wanted him, *and then* she'd thought he didn't care as much as she did! She'd even believed for a little while that he might be fighting his feelings...

She'd been *half right*, hadn't she? He'd been fighting, all right—fighting his way through all the lies he felt he had to tell her because he wasn't prepared to let her *choose* for herself.

How dared he?

Dragging a ragged breath into her aching lungs, she forced her blurred gaze to lock with his. 'You've lied to me every step of the way since the very day we met. How could y—?'

'What the hell was I supposed to do? Shake your hand and say, "Hi, I'm Ronan and in a few years I'll be blind"? Now there's a chat-up line! I should carry a tin for money and rattle it under people's noses, should I?'

Raising his voice wasn't one of his better moves, even if the bitterness in his words was like a blunt knife forced into her aching chest. 'Of course I'm not suggesting that! But you took the choice from me—how can you not know that? It's what you've done all along—with *everything*! Like I'm some weak, defenceless female who can't handle anything—is that how you *see me*?'

He roared down at her. 'Yes, because you're taking the news so well right now, aren't you?'

'I'm not taking it well right now because you've *hidden this from me*!' How could he be this stupid?

'Stop it!' The dangerous level of white-hot fury told her just how much he'd been holding inside. 'What did you expect me to do, Kerry? You're a giver—you've given everything up for other people your whole life! I'm not adding my name to the list—*full stop*. I'm no one's sympathy case!'

Her voice rose in reaction to his. 'And you've seen that as my weakness all along, haven't you? Well, let me tell you something, Ronan O'Keefe—you don't know me anywhere near as well as you think you do! Because I *am* the strong one in my family—I'm the one that holds it all together— I'm the one that's there when the rest of them need support or advice or someone to take the weight when they have problems elsewhere. And if you think some weak, pathetic female can do all that, then you're even more of an idiot than you are for thinking you can just go lock yourself in a room and stagnate. You'll go insane and you know fine well you will!'

'You don't know anything about the plans I've made.'

She laughed, but it was still laced with anger. 'I know whatever they are they involve you making some of the most universally stupid decisions ever made!'

'Like letting you be the strong one for me and making you give up even more of your own dreams to do it, you mean?' He stepped forwards, his eyes flashing. 'You may have been the strong one for your family, Kerry—but it came at a cost, didn't it? And now I'm supposed to roll over and play dead while you do the same thing for me?'

Kerry lifted her chin. 'It was my choice to make. And that's the one thing you've not given me: *a choice*. If you care even the least little bit about me, then you'd want me to have what I want.'

'Haven't I wanted to give you everything you want the whole way through this?'

'Including *you?*' Her eyes widened in amazement. 'You gave yourself to me *for me,* did you? The poor woman who needed a holiday affair to liven up her sad life?'

Ronan looked as if he were about to explode. 'I gave in because I couldn't stop myself from wanting you more than I've ever wanted anyone or anything my entire life!'

'But not enough to trust me.' She shook her head and looked back at the river, unable to believe what he was saying to her. Her heart still thundering, she looked way down deep inside for the strength to force calmness into her voice. 'I had no idea you had so low an opinion of me.'

She glanced at him from the corner of her eye, just in time to see him rock right back on his heels, swearing enough to turn the air blue around them before he glared at her. 'This has *nothing* to do with *you*! I make my own choices—no one else does it for me.'

Despite how badly she was shaking, she managed to smile cruelly at him. 'Oh, yes, you've made that more than clear—thank you. This had *nothing* to do with me.'

He'd had no intention of letting her in from the beginning, had he? He wasn't letting anyone in. His own private hell; no room for anyone else—least of all a woman incapable of loving him enough to see him as more than just his ability to see.

Did he honestly think she'd have reacted like this if she hadn't loved him as much as she did?

Ronan was fighting to get control of himself, sucking in deep breaths of air, his hands on his hips, head tilted back, and after a long while his chin dropped and his gaze collided with hers. 'I can't hold two of us together through this. I'll have enough to adjust to.'

'You selfish son of a—'

The flat tone tugged hard on the thread he was holding onto his anger with. 'I'm *selfish* for not wanting you to give up your life to nursemaid me? Tell me exactly how that one works.'

'So you did this for me 'cos I'm the kind of woman who's not strong enough to love you for better or worse? Or you did it for you, 'cos I'm the kind of woman who might force herself to love you because she feels sorry for you? Either way I fall woefully short, don't I? You've decided I'm incapable of loving you because you're you, haven't you? I'm not allowed to look you in the eye and decide for myself if I want to spend the rest of my life with you no matter what life throws our way? How dare you decide what I can and can't feel? *How dare you?*'

With every sentence the tears were flowing hotter and faster and thicker down her cheeks. How could he think that? He really didn't care about her one iota as much as she'd grown to care for him.

And that was that. There was no more. The journey was over.

He didn't love her.

When he clenched his jaw, his hands hanging in fists by his side the way they had when she'd pushed him on the island, she stepped back—because she wasn't pushing any more. There was no point.

He stepped forwards.

'Don't come near me, Ronan.' She reached up and used her sleeves to swipe her cheeks dry, blankly noticing that she still had the headache tablets in her hand. Just as well, really—she was going to need them.

She couldn't bear to look at him again; it just hurt too much. So she turned on her heel and walked away. Not even thinking about whether or not he was following until a last thought occurred to her and she turned round with her chin held high as she walked back.

Ronan was standing statue-still, fierce, blistering anger radiating from him as she cleared her throat.

'One more thing: if our places were switched—if it was me that was losing my sight and you were in love with me— would you stay with me out of pity? Or would me loving you back have been enough?' She felt herself welling up all over again. 'Would you hate me if I pulled the stunt you just have? As much as I hate you right now? Because if you'd have given me the choice I wouldn't necessarily have chosen you, Ronan—but I might have picked *us*. For a while it felt like together we ruled the world. That's how it felt when there was an "us". But there never was an "us" was there?'

She laughed what felt distinctly like her last laugh; it didn't even sound that genuine to her own ears.

'You decided that and now we'll never know what I would have chosen. I take it back; I'm not glad I met you.' She nodded to confirm it as she turned away for the last time. 'I wish I never had.'

CHAPTER ELEVEN

IT TOOK a long time for Ronan to get past his anger enough to believe with any degree of conviction Kerry mightn't have meant some of the things she'd thrown at him; many of them which, with hindsight, he knew he'd deserved.

'I'm not glad I met you. I wish I never had.'

He knew *he* didn't feel that way. There was no way he would trade his time with Kerry. She'd been the best thing to happen to him in a long while; ever since he'd first started to notice the change in his vision during the day and had to admit it was finally happening. Since then he'd felt as if he were walking around with a hammer hanging over his head; being with Kerry had made him forget, at least for a while. With her, he'd been more alive—had smiled more, laughed more, wanted to pack even more into his days. She'd been like the sun to him. And he'd naturally turned towards that brightness while darkness was creeping in everywhere else. No, he wasn't the least little bit sorry he'd met her. But he was sorry he'd hurt her so badly and that she'd got so many things wrong when she was yelling at him…

But that didn't mean he'd shake off such firmly held convictions without putting up a fight.

So he walked while he thought—at first to shake off the

boiling anger, and then, when that gradually subsided, to go through everything she'd said. It was what Paris was meant for, after all. Well, that and the most obvious other thing, of course—which just rubbed salt in the wound when he was constantly surrounded by couples all happily in love.

What would he have done if she'd been in his shoes?

It had never once occurred to him to look at it that way. Why? He'd been so damn busy doing what he thought was the right thing, that was why. And she'd figured out every single little clue in the last ten odd weeks in the space of about half an hour—known exactly what he'd been doing—which just proved he'd been right all those times when he'd thought she could see inside him.

It was reassuring to know he could be right about *something*—because she'd taken every other thing that had made perfect sense to him up until a couple of hours ago and thrown it in the flipping river. *Women.* Whose idea was it to make them so intuitive? Seemed like an unfair advantage in the battle of the sexes to him.

And, yes, she was right—he had had to be devious. But what did she expect him to do? It wasn't as if he ran all over the world advertising his problems. Who did that anyway?

But she had no idea what she'd be taking on with him. Not just that he'd be reliant on her for more things than he would want to be, but that he'd not exactly be the easiest guy to live with when it happened. *He knew him.* There were going to be days when he'd be a bear and days when he'd be better left to wallow—not that he planned on allowing himself too much of the latter, mind you.

As to the locking himself in a room to stagnate… Like hell. He'd had years to think about how he'd live his new life when the old one was taken from him. And he'd made plans to stay as busy and active and productive as humanly possible—not as if he'd not still be *him*, was it? He'd just be a toned-down version.

But the way he'd looked at it, he'd already packed more into ten years than many people did into a lifetime.

'Grooming her' to take his place was an accusation pretty close to the mark, though. He might have to give a little on that. But she'd loved so many of the places he'd loved that it had made sense to him to pass on some of what he knew. And she had a world full of adventures ahead of her. Why wouldn't he want to encourage her to take them? So it therefore followed he'd try and help any way he could.

Maybe he'd not have to give all that much on that one, after all…

Mind you—he hadn't expected to have her turn it round so all of his reasoning came down to her being lacking in something in his eyes. *And selfish?* Selfish for not letting her in? It made him laugh; selfish had been wanting her as much as he had. How could she not see that?

Venus and Mars.

But he'd not had a chance to make any of those points or say any of those things to Kerry. Or so many other things that needed to be said. He just prayed she wouldn't get as upset as she'd been again. *Ever again.* It had been the worst experience of his life seeing her like that: so anguished—for him. *Broken*—and he'd been the one to break her. He'd watched the bright, beautiful, spirited, strong-willed, intelligent woman he loved crumble before his eyes. And he'd done that to her. He didn't know if he could ever forgive himself for that.

The only thing he knew for certain was he couldn't leave it the way it had been left. She wanted the right to choose. Then that meant he'd have to lay it all on the line for her. *All of it.*

No more lying—to her or to himself.

So after three hours of wandering he went looking for her. With no initial idea of where he'd find her, which frankly had panicked him a bit, until he remembered why they were in Paris in the first place. If she wasn't there he'd try the hotel, search the whole city if he had to and lay siege at the airport as a last resort.

Trouble was, the Jardin du Luxembourg wasn't exactly the size of someone's back garden. So when he would look back on it in the future he'd have to put it down to luck that he found her sitting on a metal chair by the Fontaine de Médicis, surrounded by hundreds of shades of autumn leaves in russets and browns and golds above her head, under her feet and reflected in the mirrored surface of the water—all the shades he loved in her eyes—and bright sunshine shining on her face; Kerry Doyle in her natural habitat.

She lifted her chin as he approached and he watched her while she watched him—the air of tension lying between them palpable even from twenty feet away. And the fact that the light seemed to have died inside her slayed him—it really did. *He'd done that.*

Her breasts rose and fell with a deep breath when he was closer, her voice holding the soft husky, edge that had always got to him most.

'What do you want, Ronan?'

'You knew I'd come find you.'

'Why would I know that?'

He frowned. How could she think he wouldn't?

'And sitting here looking back on everything I've started to see things more clearly. I get it all now. There's nothing else you need to say to me.'

'What exactly do you see more clearly?' He stood with his back to the ornate fencing and huge mounted concrete jardinières, not ready to pull up a chair beside her while he had a suspicion he might not like the answer to his question.

He was right.

'I was thinking about all the times way back at the beginning when you would take my elbow or hold my hand—like you did in New York. At the time I thought you did it because you liked touching me, but now I'm wondering if you just did it—'

Ronan clenched his teeth when he realized where she was going. 'Because I needed to rather than because I wanted to?'

Kerry simply looked up at him, her gaze tangling with his and a deep, empty sadness filling her eyes.

Ronan folded his arms across his chest before glowering down at her. 'Thanks for that—but it had more to do with the fact I haven't been able to stop touching you since the day we met. It's something I've never had any control over no matter how hard I tried.'

'Well, that's what I hoped once, but the longer I had to think about this now I know everything, the more time there is for paranoia to set in.' She shrugged and looked away from his face, the very visible lack of fight in her enough to make him want to shake her back to life. Having her yell had been better than this.

He clenched his jaw and took a breath, unable to take his eyes off her in case she disappeared again and he didn't get a second chance.

'I didn't plan for any of this to happen.'

She cocked a brow and looked at him from the corner of her eye. 'Oh, that's not true, now, is it?'

'I meant us. I didn't plan for an "us".'

'There isn't an "us".'

Ronan took a deep breath. 'Yes, there is. If there wasn't, would I be here?'

The confession didn't get her to look at him and it was

enough to make Ronan fearful that he'd already done too much damage. Though the fact she sat back a little and wrapped her arms around her middle was enough for him to hope she was holding her emotions inside—probably because she'd let so much out already, and maybe partly because he'd given her such a hard time about not being strong last time. When, actually, a sign of some emotion might have helped around about now…

He couldn't keep changing his mind, though, could he? 'I've known since I was a kid that one day I'd lose my sight— it's hereditary, carried down the female side to the male. Once it happens in your family a couple of times they know to look for it. My kids would all be able to see but my daughter's son's might not. And sometimes the boys will be blind when they're little, sometimes it happens later—I'm one of the lucky ones. My sisters are all carriers but thankfully so far they've only had girls.'

Kerry didn't say anything, didn't move.

So with a heartfelt sigh, Ronan stepped to the side, grabbing hold of a chair and dragging it over to sit, he rested his forearms on his knees and focussed on her profile, his tone still low.

'I was in New York to see a specialist. Knew it was a long shot, but had to try. And I have made plans for when I can't see any more and none of them involve me locking myself away in a room somewhere—just so you know. I planned on using this trip to see as many people as I could while I still can, but not because I don't plan on ever hearing their voices again.' His chest tightened when he saw the first tear streak silently down her cheek, her eyes still focussed on some random point straight ahead of her. 'I've made lots of plans because I knew I had to. I was prepared.'

Kerry's throat convulsed.

And Ronan's voice deepened as he made the biggest confession. 'I wasn't prepared for a you.'

God, he hated that she was so silent. It wasn't like his Kerry to be so quiet and distant. He studied the top of her head, where the bright sunshine was picking out strands of red in amongst the deep chestnut—his gaze then following the waves down the side of her face.

'I don't think you're weak, by the way. You're confident, full of life, fun to be around, sassy and too flipping smart for your own good, but you're not weak. And you're adventurous. You set off to travel around the world on your own and I think that would make your nana very proud. If you stick with me, then at some point I won't have any choice but to hold you back from some of the adventures you can take. And I couldn't live with that. Especially not when I've taken most of those adventures myself. I know what you'd be missing out on.'

'But that's not your choice to make.'

At least it got a reaction, 'Maybe not.'

And that earned him a sideways glare. 'No maybe in it. I'm the only one who gets to choose where I go to and when and how and with who. Just because I've let you lead me around the world doesn't mean I wouldn't have managed a version of it on my own. I went with you because I *chose* to go with you. That doesn't mean you'd get to tell me where and when in the future.'

The very mention of the word 'future' was enough to give him a little more hope. 'Okay.'

The one-word reply got her to look at him. And when she did she frowned, rapidly swiping the two lonely tears off her cheeks as she continued—as if by backing down on one thing he'd opened a floodgate.

'You don't know me well enough to know what I can and can't cope with. And even when you do, don't for one second presume that I might not have untapped inner strength yet to be found.'

Letting his gaze trail over her face, he took another breath. 'You have no idea what you'd be taking on with me. I—'

'You might find I have more of an idea than you think I do.' Her chin rose. 'And you *really* need to stop telling me what I can and can't do.'

He smiled a small smile at that, forcing it away to continue, 'I was going to say I'm hard work. And the way I've been on this trip with you isn't how I always am—there are days when I don't do so well with this and—'

'I'm not the least bit surprised. I'd be angry at the world if it was me. And I'd wallow. And I'd be scared—not that I think you're likely to ever confess to that one. Though I'm probably not as much work as you can be, even on this trip—'cos you weren't always that easy, as it happens.' She almost smiled.

And it dragged a rueful smile onto his mouth. 'I tried not to complicate things, if you remember.'

'Not lying would have been one way of helping with that, don't you think?'

'It was a lie of omission—it wasn't ever meant to hurt you. Like I said, I wasn't prepared for a you…'

Kerry's shoulders relaxed a little, her gaze dropping to the usual spot at the base of his neck as she drew in another deep breath, her voice softening. 'I wasn't exactly prepared for a you either. But you could have told me, Ronan. I wish you'd believed in me.'

He waited until her lashes rose. 'I thought I was doing the right thing—for both of us.'

'You were wrong.'

'Well, duh.' He tried a warmer smile on for size, holding his breath until she smiled back at him. 'I finally understood that when you asked me what I'd have done if it was you in my shoes.'

The suggestion of light in Kerry's eyes made his chest tighten. 'And what would you have done?'

'Probably been just as angry at you as you were at me when I realized you'd hidden it…'

She quirked her brows in a way that simply said, *see*, and it was enough to get him to continue.

'And I wouldn't have let you go. Not ever.'

It took a second, a half-dozen different emotions clouding her eyes. And then the light switched on inside her, lighting her face and softening her eyes to a warm glow. 'You could just take a shot at telling me you love me, you know.'

'It wasn't as simple as that, there were—'

'Yes, it was, you idiot. It's exactly that simple. It's the only thing that really matters.'

Breathing evenly became a bit of an effort for him, his chin dropping and a frown appearing on his face as he tried to find the right words to make her understand.

'You still don't get it. It's not you that's the weak one here, Kerry—it's me, and I *hate* that,' He pursed his lips into a flat line and forced his chin back up. 'I'll need you more than you need me.'

Her voice was filled with infinite patience, 'Listen up, genius—if you think I don't need you every bit as much as you need me, then you're sorely mistaken. I *do* need you.'

'I love that you're as open and giving as you are, Kerry, it's just—'

Her eyes sparkled. 'Careful—you almost said it.'

The sigh was one of exasperation this time. 'Is there any chance of me getting to complete a sentence? I'm trying to explain here.'

'If you'd just tell me you love me then I could say I love you too and we'd be done. Then we could get to the good stuff.'

There was a long moment of silence when he paused for breath, her words swirling in around him like a blanket, muffling out the rest of the world until she was all there was—which left him floundering for more words when she leaned forwards and rested her forearms on her knees, her face close to his.

'You done now?'

Pretty much, but, 'I can't see you go through what you went through today. It was hell to watch.'

'I only went through that today because it was such a shock—I didn't see it coming. I missed all the signs. And, loving you as much as I do, the thought that you've felt the need to hide so much from me *killed me*. That's all.' And she'd said all of it in a calm, sweetly soft tone with only the faintest shimmering in her eyes—she even shrugged her shoulders at the end.

It almost made him believe her. 'So you're fine with it now, are you?'

'No, I'm not fine with it. What kind of a stupid question is that?' She scowled at him. 'I hate that this is happening to you. *I hate it.* But I can't stop it, can I? I'm assuming, knowing you, that if there was a way to fix it then you'd have found it.'

'It wouldn't be for want of trying, no.'

She nodded. 'Then there's nothing we can do.'

We. How could such a tiny word completely cripple him emotionally? He swallowed hard, dropping his gaze to her fine-boned hands and fighting the need to reach for them. 'And that's that, then—you won't break down on me again like you did today? 'Cos, seriously—you might be strong enough to go through it again, but I'm not so sure I can take it on a regular basis.'

Her hands reached across and took his, fingers tangling and

squeezing. 'Happy tears only. That's the best I can promise you. Though for the record—it would help lots if you never held anything back from me ever again and if I ever get upset over anything else you could just hold me and I'd feel better. Or you could kiss it better for me.'

Ronan's mouth twitched. 'Worked before.'

'It did. Almost worth squeezing a few tears out for…'

He chuckled, lifting his chin to look into her dancing eyes. '*Woman*…don't you *dare* play me…'

'You'd catch me on it if I did.'

'I would.'

'Okay.' With an impish smile and her face lit up with the inner glow he loved best, she wriggled further forwards on her chair until her knees hit his. 'I'm gonna throw some stuff in here before you start to work through any of the other feeble excuses you have for attempting to stop me choosing to be with you.'

'You've got remarkably confident for someone who'd convinced themselves they were being used as a guide dog not that long ago.'

'Blind jokes. *Funny*.' She scowled at him. 'And paranoia like that only set in 'cos I'd convinced myself you didn't love me—because if you had you'd have trusted me. Now I understand your twisted logic came partly from the fact that you *do* love me. And do you want to know why I'm so sure you do—apart from the obvious fact that you came looking for me to talk this through, that is?'

'I'm pretty sure you're going to tell me.'

He got a firm nod. 'You have to, you see, because I couldn't love you to the pit of my soul the way I do if you weren't the right one for me. And if you're the right one for me then you have no choice but to feel the same way back. That's how it works. I'm your one in six billion—you're mine. But you should know that already when you've been all over the entire planet and never bumped into me before now.'

There was a very Kerry sense of logic in there that made complete sense to him. Even if it was proof positive of what he'd known for a long time. 'I'm still standing by the fact you're more than a little crazy.'

An arched brow quirked. 'Our fathers play golf together, for crying out loud. If we weren't meant to meet when we did, then don't you think we'd have at least *known* about each other before?'

Actually he didn't have an answer for that one.

'That's what I thought too. This was meant to happen. You just messed up the great scheme of things by not believing in it. Whereas I was the one racking her brain for weeks trying to find a way to make it work…'

He smiled affectionately. Getting told off by Kerry wasn't all that bad really. Not now he knew they were going to be all right. Because they were, weren't they?

'Now—let's just talk about the travelling thing, shall we? You have me all trained up so there's plenty of adventures to be had—*together*. You know all the best places to go and you can tell me where and how to get there, because you have this innate talent for retaining all kinds of details in your head—a veritable walking encyclopedia, in fact. And I know you're going to try and tell me there'll come a point when you can't do all the things you can do now but you can't say—'

'I didn't say I was giving it up. You assumed I was. When I met up with the friends I did it was only to let them know it might be a long time before I saw them again—and I wanted to *see* them while I still could, that's all.' He took another breath. 'But I wasn't about to have you jump up and volunteer to hold my hand when—'

'Ronan, I love holding your hand. I've been holding your hand since our first day together. I'm holding your hands now. I'm not going to stop doing it just because something else changes. I *love* you. And when you love someone you hold their hand. It's a sign of affection.'

'You are the bossiest woman I've ever met. Have you finished lecturing me yet?'

'After the stunt you tried pulling?' She laughed in disbelief. 'You have years of this coming, mister.'

Then she leaned in and pressed a swift kiss on his lips, 'You just hate that I'm making sense when you've spent so long telling yourself this could never work.'

If she'd shut up for five minutes he might get to tell her he'd had some changes of heart on that subject. Truth was, if he was honest, he would never have come looking for her if he hadn't wanted to find a way to make it work. But then he was a *weak man* when it came to Kerry; he always had been…

'That long list of things you said I was: confident, fun, adventurous—'

'Sassy…' he mumbled under his breath.

'Yes, those.' She smiled warmly at him, her heart in her eyes. 'You need to know it's you that brings all that out in me. It may always have been there but with you I'm— *more*—more of everything. Without you I'd be *less*. That's why I need you.'

'Less sassy is fine with me.'

'And you made me paint again.' This time her eyes shimmered suspiciously enough to make him frown again. 'Lord, but I loved you for that. I should never have let it slide. But now I have it back and, since I was sat here in this park with plenty of time to think, I have a theory on how we could use that too…'

His chin dropped to his chest with a groan. 'I'm never

leaving you on your own for this long ever again if it gives you this much time to prove a point you've already made.'

Soft musical laughter sounded above his head. 'I'm very glad to hear it. I'm never leaving you either.'

'Well, could we hurry up and get to the good stuff, then, do you think?' He smiled down at their hands.

She let go of his hands and framed his face, tilting his chin back up so she could look in his eyes the way she did that made him feel she could see inside him, her voice seductively low and filled with emotion.

'Close your eyes for me.'

'Why?'

'Do I have to blindfold you?'

'Blindfold for the guy who's losing his sight—that's considerate. I *feel* loved now.'

Kerry scowled fiercely. 'We need to talk about the blind jokes at some point.'

'Later.' He closed his eyes. 'Happy now?'

'Can you still see me?'

Oh, she knew how to take his heart and scrunch it up into a little tiny ball, didn't she?

He had to clear his throat to speak. 'I can always see you. I told you that once before.'

Since he'd met her she was all he could see—in the daylight when he couldn't stop looking at her, and when he was in the darkness, whether awake or on the fringes of sleep. She was all he saw.

He lifted one of her hands off his face and set it flat against his chest, covering it with his own. 'I see you with this. Your hair is a really deep chestnut and it does this sexy curly thing all around your face. Your eyes remind me of autumn. And you're smiling that way that makes it look like you're lit up from inside. I see you. And that's before I go into all the things I see inside you; you're amazing. I've thought that from the get go.'

He heard her take a shaky breath, her voice filled with emotion. 'Then you see me better than anyone else ever has.'

'They weren't looking properly. We going-blind types tend to pay more attention than most…'

Soft lips brushed across his, her sweet breath whispering over his face. 'You really need to learn that being nice doesn't need to be disguised under something flippant, you know. We'll work on that. Now tell me what you can hear.'

Ronan knew what she was doing—and there was barely enough room left in his chest for his lungs to work properly. 'Your voice—you breathing—my heart beating loud, if we're being honest.'

'We are from here on in and don't you forget it. What else?'

'Leaves rustling.' He tried to nail each sound down one by one. 'The fountain—birds—'

He smiled as he got more. 'Wind in the leaves still left on the trees—kids laughing somewhere. Damn, I'm good at this.'

'Keep going.'

He dropped both hands to her jean-clad thighs; up over her hips to her waist where he spread his fingers wide and squeezed tight. 'I can smell damp leaves on the ground and the water behind me and that scent that's always been Kerry, Kerry Doyle to me. Gotta love that scent, really…'

It earned him another kiss, words vibrating against his mouth. 'Still incorrigible. I love you, you idiot.'

Men didn't cry. But if they did he would have when his heart swelled to bursting point. Because he suddenly knew what she was going to say about the painting. 'Now you're going to fill in the rest for me, aren't you? With lots of references to impressionist paintings…'

There was only a heartbeat of a pause. 'The sky above us

is a light, bright pale blue. Think about looking from the window of a plane and how far it stretches out—then add clouds so thin you can see little pieces of the sky through them. And they're drifting so you know there's more of a breeze higher up than there is down here. Like that time we lay on the beach in Fiji and watched them go by for hours on end…'

Ronan's hands tightened as she continued in the richly warm, slightly husky voice he loved so very much. 'All around us there are trees, leaves turning all the colours of autumn—brown and russet and red and ochre and gold all mixed together. You can see the sky through them in places. Paris at the Fontaine de Médicis is your reference for autumn from today on…'

For the rest of his days when he thought of autumn he would think of finding Kerry surrounded by those trees. And he'd think of the colours in her eyes. She was clever, his woman—taking hints of the things they'd seen together to help paint the picture inside his mind. Showing him she could be his eyes when he couldn't see any more. How had he thought for one second he could live without her in his life?

'It reminds me more of a Van Gogh than a Monet, but we might need to see more paintings for you to get the references from art…'

Ronan had to clear his throat. 'You're doing fine.'

Her voice lowered again, soft and intimate like it was when they talked on a plane or after making love, when they would lie side by side in the darkness at night laughing and sharing the way only they did. 'You see—it's another sign that I was always meant for you, me loving art from when I was little. My mother taught me all the names of the colours so one day I could tell you what they are. I just had to get on the right plane at the right time to find you, that's all. And now it all makes sense. You brought bright, vibrant colour into my life—all I'll be doing is giving it back to you.'

A sound distinctly like a laughed sob made him open his eyes. And Kerry was so close he could see the tears forming in her beautiful eyes, his throat clogging up and his vision blurring, his voice rough.

'I love you. More than I could ever begin to tell you.'

She sobbed a husky chuckle of laughter. 'I know.'

When he swallowed hard she leaned in closer and searched his eyes. 'Are those happy tears?'

Ronan sat a little taller, frowning at her. 'Like hell. It's the wind here—it's sharp.'

Kerry pursed her lips and nodded. 'Mmm-hmm.'

He leaned in and kissed away the 'happy tears' he could see in her eyes before nudging the end of his nose on hers, gruffly informing her, 'You better marry me, then.'

Kerry nodded. 'I better had.'

'Honeymoon in Kenya do?'

Her face lit up with the excitement he loved to invoke in her, her nodding firm. 'Absolutely.'

The hands on her waist smoothed up her back to press her closer to his chest, his voice rumbling over her lips. 'Good— 'cos I have a flight booked at the beginning of the month.'

Kerry jumped back a little. 'I can't organize a wedding in less than a month!'

'Yes, you can. We worked on spur-of-the-moment, remember?' He moved in for another kiss.

But Kerry leaned out of the way. 'A month isn't spur-of-the-moment! It's make-Kerry-crazy.'

'We got that one covered—' he pressed against her back more firmly and lifted his other hand to the back of her head to stop her getting away '—and I have a venue in mind that'll fulfil the fantasy for you—trust me. Then we can tick that one off the list too.'

'*You* tick all my fantasies.'

He didn't waste time on another word. Instead he showed her how much he loved her by kissing her until she went limp and languid against him. Only then did he lift his head, smiling contentedly down at her heavy-lidded eyes and answering drunken smile.

'And I get to meet Nana. Think I can get her to love me as much as you do?'

Kerry's lower lip trembled. 'Oh, she'll love you, all right. And she'll have plenty of helpful words of wisdom too— most likely with a lecture when I tell her what it took to get us to here. You wait and see…'

'I'm looking forward to it.'

'One more thing.'

'There always is with you.'

'I should tell you about the hereditary thing that runs in *my* side of the family.' When he stiffened she moved in to slide her mouth over his, stage-whispering the rest. 'Three generations of twins now, you know…'

'You have got to be ki—'

EPILOGUE

A WEDDING could indeed be planned in less than a month. Though Kerry would always wonder just how they managed it. But with determination, teamwork, Ronan's enthusiastic imagination and Kerry's organizational skills it all went off without a hitch.

Mind you—marrying a millionaire determined to make things happen no matter how much it cost to *make them happen* helped.

She married him wearing Nana's beautiful nineteen-twenties rose silk wedding dress complete with antique wax flower headpiece and floor-length veil and all the way through the ceremony Ronan's stunning eyes shone at her, making her glow from head to toe.

And he hadn't done too badly with their location either, not that Kerry would have expected anything less now she knew him so well…

Something certain members of her family doubted she could after a mere three months. But then, much to Ronan's deep chuckling amusement, she'd pointed out that they'd spent one thousand eight hundred and forty-eight hours together pretty much constantly one on one. And if that was split down into normal 'dating' hours then technically they'd been seeing each other about a year and a half. So if a couple were as much in love as they were after a year and a half and they decided to get married then the rest of the world wouldn't have a problem with it, *would they?*

'You forgot to stick your tongue out and say "so there",' he pointed out afterwards.

'Ooh, don't think for a second I wasn't tempted!'

They had pictures taken on lawns sprinkled with autumn leaves in the grounds of Kinnitty Castle; a gothic revival castle at the foothills of the Slieve Bloom Mountains near where Ronan had grown up. Because flowers and dresses and 'girl stuff' were all hers, he calmly informed her, but the role of 'fantasy fulfiller'—*'all mine and always will be'*.

And in the spirit of 'surprises' he'd even managed to keep the location from her up until the week before, something Kerry didn't have any complaints about with the faith she had in his ability to make her happy—especially when they were sitting in the Great Hall of the O'Carrolls for a banquet in spectacular fantasy setting: crisp white linen softly finished with luxurious green centre runners complemented by the green chair bands on champagne seat covers and the lilting music of an Irish harp weaving a spell over their families and friends.

It was the stuff of dreams.

Though they were probably the only wedding reception on the face of the earth with about ten choices of dessert— because Ronan didn't see why he had to choose *one* when they could have a little of *all of them*…

And Kerry made it through the entire day without crying— almost.

It was when they went to see Nana before the dancing began that did it. Because with both of them hunching down in front of her, one of each of her small crinkled hands on their faces and Ronan thanking her for sending Kerry out into the world to 'find him' when he needed her most, so much emotion welled up in Kerry's chest that it had to go *somewhere*…

But then when he found out Kerry had only been at the fountain in Paris because that was where her grandfather had proposed to Nana he said straight away it made even more sense to him they'd found their own happy ending there.

'Not ending, you idiot—*beginning*.' Kerry smiled before kissing him for saying it.

He squeezed the fingers tangled in his, the band of her wedding ring pressing between them. 'Oh, no, you don't—*stop that*.'

'What's she doing?' Nana turned her head.

'She's about to cry and ruin her make-up. You should speak to her—she never listens to me.'

Nana laughed throatily the way Kerry loved most. It had always been an indication of her wicked sense of humour, that dirty laugh of hers. 'Looks beautiful in my dress, though, doesn't she?'

Ronan's deep voice huskily rumbled the answer, his sensational eyes glowing with deeply felt emotion. 'She does. *Very beautiful*.'

'Tell me what she looks like, Ronan.'

So he did, describing every last detail in the same husky tone and making Kerry smile through her tears—*happy tears*—because she'd *never* been happier.

She mouthed the words at him. *I love you.*

And his fingers squeezed again, chin lifting before he smiled the most sinfully sexy slow smile and mouthed back, *Love you too. Woman.*

It was the only thing that really mattered.

* * * * *

Chapter 1

October
New York City

Nicole Masters was sitting cross-legged on her sofa while a cold autumn rain peppered the windows of her fourth-floor apartment. She was poking at the ice cream in her bowl and trying not to be in a mood.

Six weeks ago, a simple trip to her neighborhood pharmacy had turned into a nightmare. She'd walked into the middle of a robbery. She never even saw the man who shot her in the head and left her for dead. She'd survived, but some of her senses had not. She was dealing with short-term memory loss and a tendency to stagger. Even though she'd been told the problems were most likely temporary, she waged a daily battle with depression.

Her parents had been killed in a car wreck when she was twenty-one. And except for a few friends—and most recently her boyfriend, Dominic Tucci, who lived in the apartment right above hers, she was alone. Her doctor kept reminding her that she should be grateful to be alive, and on one level she knew he was right. But he wasn't living in her shoes.

If she'd been anywhere else but at that pharmacy when the robbery happened, she wouldn't have died twice on the way to the hospital. Instead of being grateful that she'd survived, she couldn't stop thinking of what she'd lost.

But that wasn't the end of her troubles. On top of everything else, something strange was happening inside her head. She'd begun to hear odd things: sounds, not voices—at least, she didn't think it was voices. It was more like the distant noise of rapids—a rush of wind and water inside her head that, when it came, blocked out everything around her. It didn't happen often, but when it did, it was frightening, and it was driving her crazy.

The blank moments, which is what she called them, even had a rhythm. First there came that sound, then a cold sweat, then panic with no reason. Part of her feared it was the beginning of an emotional breakdown. And part of her feared it wasn't—that it was going to turn out to be a permanent souvenir of her resurrection.

Frustrated with herself and the situation as it stood, she upped the sound on the TV remote. But instead of *Wheel of Fortune,* an announcer broke in with a special bulletin.

"This just in. Police are on the scene of a kidnapping that occurred only hours ago at The Dakota. Molly Dane, the six-year-old daughter of one of Hollywood's blockbuster stars, Lyla Dane, was taken by force from the family apartment. At this time they have yet to receive a ransom demand. The housekeeper was seriously injured during the abduction, and is, at the present time, in surgery. Police are hoping to be able to talk to her once she regains consciousness. In the meantime, we are going now to a press conference with Lyla Dane."

Horrified, Nicole stilled as the cameras went live to where the actress was speaking before a bank of microphones. The shock and terror in Lyla Dane's voice were physically painful to watch. But even though Nicole kept upping the volume, the sound continued to fade.

Just when she was beginning to think something was wrong with her set, the broadcast suddenly switched from the Dane press conference to what appeared to be footage of the kidnapping, beginning with footage from inside the apartment.

When the front door suddenly flew back against the wall and four men rushed in, Nicole gasped. Horrified, she quickly realized that this must have been caught on a security camera inside the Dane apartment.

As Nicole continued to watch, a small Asian woman, who she guessed was the maid, rushed forward in an effort to keep them out. When one of the men hit her in the face with his gun, Nicole moaned. The violence was too reminiscent of what she'd lived through. Sick to her stomach, she fisted her hands against her belly, wishing it was over, but unable to tear her gaze away.

When the maid dropped to the carpet, the same man followed with a vicious kick to the little woman's midsection that lifted her off the floor.

"Oh, my God," Nicole said. When blood began to pool beneath the maid's head, she started to cry.

As the tape played on, the four men split up in different directions. The camera caught one running down a long marble hallway, then disappearing into a room. Moments later he reappeared, carrying a little girl, who Nicole assumed was Molly Dane. The child was wearing a pair of red pants and a white turtleneck sweater, and her hair was partially blocking her abductor's face as he carried her down the hall. She was kicking and screaming in his arms, and when he slapped her, it elicited an agonized scream that brought the other three running. Nicole watched in horror as one of them ran up and put his hand over Molly's face. Seconds later, she went limp.

One moment they were in the foyer, then they were gone.

Nicole jumped to her feet, then staggered drunkenly. The bowl of ice cream she'd absentmindedly placed in her lap shattered at her feet, splattering glass and melting ice cream everywhere.

The picture on the screen abruptly switched from the kidnapping to what Nicole assumed was a rerun of Lyla Dane's plea for her daughter's safe return, but she was numb.

Before she could think what to do next, the doorbell rang. Startled by the unexpected sound, she shakily swiped at the tears and took a step forward. She didn't feel the glass shards piercing her feet until she took the second step. At that point, sharp pains shot through her foot. She gasped, then looked down in confusion. Her legs looked as if she'd been running through mud, and she was standing in broken glass and ice cream, while a thin ribbon of blood seeped out from beneath her toes.

"Oh, no," Nicole mumbled, then stifled a second moan of pain.

The doorbell rang again. She shivered, then clutched her head in confusion.

"Just a minute!" she yelled, then tried to sidestep the rest of the debris as she hobbled to the door.

When she looked through the peephole in the door, she didn't know whether to be relieved or regretful.

It was Dominic, and as usual, she was a mess.

Nicole smiled a little self-consciously as she opened the door to let him in. "I just don't know what's happening to me. I think I'm losing my mind."

"Hey, don't talk about my woman like that."

Nicole rode the surge of delight his words brought. "So I'm still your woman?"

Dominic lowered his head.

Their lips met.

The kiss proceeded.
Slowly.
Thoroughly.

* * * * *

Be sure to look for the AFTERSHOCK *anthology
next month, as well as other exciting paranormal stories
from Silhouette Nocturne.
Available in October wherever books are sold.*

n o c t u r n e™

NEW YORK TIMES BESTSELLING AUTHOR

SHARON SALA

JANIS REAMES HUDSON
DEBRA COWAN

AFTERSHOCK

Three women are brought to the brink of death...
only to discover the aftershock of their trauma has
left them with unexpected and unwelcome gifts of
paranormal powers. Now each woman must learn to
accept her newfound abilities while fighting for life,
love and second chances....

Available October wherever books are sold.

www.eHarlequin.com
www.paranormalromanceblog.wordpress.com   SN61796

SPECIAL EDITION™

BRAVO FAMILY TIES

Tanner Bravo and Crystal Cerise had it bad
for each other, though they couldn't be more
different. Tanner was the type to settle down;
free-spirited Crystal wouldn't hear of it.
Now that Crystal was pregnant, would
Tanner have his way after all?

Look for

HAVING
TANNER BRAVO'S
BABY

by *USA TODAY* bestselling author
CHRISTINE RIMMER

Available in October wherever books are sold.

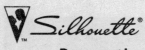

Romantic
SUSPENSE

**Sparked by Danger,
Fueled by Passion.**

USA TODAY **bestselling author**

Merline Lovelace

Undercover Wife

Secret agent Mike Callahan, code name Hawkeye,
objects when he's paired with sophisticated
Gillian Ridgeway on a dangerous spy mission
to Hong Kong. Gillian has secretly been in love
with him for years, but Hawk is an overprotective
man with a wounded past that threatens to
resurface. Now the two must put their lives—
and hearts—at risk for each other.

Available October wherever books are sold.

SRS27601

REQUEST YOUR FREE BOOKS!
2 FREE NOVELS PLUS 2
FREE GIFTS!

HARLEQUIN ROMANCE®

From the Heart, For the Heart

YES! Please send me 2 FREE Harlequin Romance® novels and my 2 FREE gifts (gifts are worth about $10). After receiving them, if I don't wish to receive any more books, I can return the shipping statement marked "cancel". If I don't cancel, I will receive 4 brand-new novels every month and be billed just $3.32 per book in the U.S. or $3.80 per book in Canada, plus 25¢ shipping and handling per book and applicable taxes, if any*. That's a savings of over 15% off the cover price! I understand that accepting the 2 free books and gifts places me under no obligation to buy anything. I can always return a shipment and cancel at any time. Even if I never buy another book, the two free books and gifts are mine to keep forever.

114 HDN ERQW 314 HDN ERQ9

Name	(PLEASE PRINT)	
Address		Apt. #
City	State/Prov.	Zip/Postal Code

Signature (if under 18, a parent or guardian must sign)

Mail to the Harlequin Reader Service:
IN U.S.A.: P.O. Box 1867, Buffalo, NY 14240-1867
IN CANADA: P.O. Box 609, Fort Erie, Ontario L2A 5X3

Not valid to current subscribers of Harlequin Romance books.

Want to try two free books from another line?
Call 1-800-873-8635 or visit www.morefreebooks.com.

* Terms and prices subject to change without notice. N.Y. residents add applicable sales tax. Canadian residents will be charged applicable provincial taxes and GST. Offer not valid in Quebec. This offer is limited to one order per household. All orders subject to approval. Credit or debit balances in a customer's account(s) may be offset by any other outstanding balance owed by or to the customer. Please allow 4 to 6 weeks for delivery. Offer available while quantities last.

Your Privacy: Harlequin Books is committed to protecting your privacy. Our Privacy Policy is available online at www.eHarlequin.com or upon request from the Reader Service. From time to time we make our lists of customers available to reputable third parties who may have a product or service of interest to you. If you would prefer we not share your name and address, please check here. ☐

HR08R

Inside ROMANCE

Stay up-to-date on all your romance reading news!

The Inside Romance newsletter is a FREE quarterly newsletter highlighting our upcoming series releases and promotions!

Click on the <u>Inside Romance</u> link on the front page of **www.eHarlequin.com** or e-mail us at insideromance@harlequin.ca to sign up to receive your FREE newsletter today!

You can also subscribe by writing us at: HARLEQUIN BOOKS Attention: Customer Service Department P.O. Box 9057, Buffalo, NY 14269-9057

Please allow 4-6 weeks for delivery of the first issue by mail.

Coming Next Month

**Handsome sheep barons, maverick tycoons and dashing princes—
you can find them all in Harlequin Romance®!**

#4051 BRIDE AT BRIAR'S RIDGE Margaret Way
In the second of the *Barons of the Outback* duet, Daniela Adami comes
to Wangaree Valley to escape her life in London. Her heart is guarded, but
when handsome sheep baron Linc Mastermann strides into her world, he
turns it upside down....

#4052 FOUND: HIS ROYAL BABY Raye Morgan
Crown Prince Dane—the third of the *Royals of Montenevada*—has heard
rumors of a secret royal baby. With the kingdom in uproar, his only choice
is to confront Alexandra Acredonna—the woman who still haunts his
dreams....

#4053 THE MILLIONAIRE'S NANNY ARRANGEMENT Linda Goodnight
Baby on Board
The only thing businessman Ryan Storm can't give his six-year-old
daughter is a mom—but he can hire the next best thing.... Pregnant and
widowed, Kelsey Mason isn't Ryan's idea of the perfect nanny—but little
Mariah bonds with her straight away, and soon he starts to fall under her
spell....

#4054 LAST-MINUTE PROPOSAL Jessica Hart
Cake-baker Tilly is taking part in a charity job-swap, but when she's paired
with ex-military chief executive Campbell Sanderson, Campbell is all hard
angles to Tilly's cozy curves. But something about her always makes him
smile. And then they share a showstopping kiss....

#4055 HIRED: THE BOSS'S BRIDE Ally Blake
9 to 5
Mitch Hanover needed a miracle—someone to bring life to his business—
and when Veronica Bing roared up in her pink Corvette and told him
she was the girl for the job, he couldn't help but agree! But even though
attraction zinged between them, Mitch had sworn never to love again....

#4056 THE SINGLE MOM AND THE TYCOON Caroline Anderson
Handsome millionaire David Cauldwell is blown away by sexy single mom
Molly Blythe. He can see she and her young son need his love as much
as he yearns for theirs—but falling in love means taking risks: David must
face the secret that changed his life....